# THE THINGS WE LEAVE BEHIND

## T.J. LEA

*For my Father. To continue to do you proud in all that I do.*

*For the friends I made that inspired the stories in this collection.*

*For the ones that left us that kept the light of this project alive.*

VELOX BOOKS

# CONTENTS

# FOREWORD

This is the second of my short story collection courtesy of Velox Books. We pick up where the first entry left off, focusing on similar subjects of loss, grief and the unknowable, but with a noted darker tone. Those of you with a weak stomach or who struggled through some of the more unpleasant parts of the previous collection may wish to take heed of what is about to come. We will also look at the claustrophobic situations involving toxic relationships, imaginary friends and deviate into the strange with talking furniture, clouds hiding an ancient dead god and shadows that have a will of their own.

Some of these stories do take place in my shared universe that is Sturgeon, a town housing all manner of nightmares and unique individuals locked in a struggle for human protection and nightmare recognition. If you enjoy this, please consider picking up my debut novella, *The Last Sin Eater*, and its subsequent entries.

Nevertheless, you are here and you chose to pick up/download my book. For that I am eternally grateful, and I hope the ride you are about to go on evokes feelings of empathy, terror, disgust and connection with your fellow person. We are all stumbling in the dark after all… It's just a matter of finding the switch before something else does.

Enjoy.

# THE THINGS WE LEAVE BEHIND

My mom was the sort of person to look like a wallflower until you got close and then spout out facts about her favourite animal. It was an emperor penguin. She said their journey for love and parenthood was the hardest and most connecting with her.

I'm told all the usual things about her: she had a smile that could light up a room, her laugh cut through the malaise of an awkward party, her stride was confident, and her form was elegant. From the day I could understand what it was to be remembered, she was painted to me as a true goddess.

After all, aren't all moms supposed to be that to their children growing up?

Mom died when I was 4. Aggressive cancer riddled her body with tumours, stole her stride, her smile, her laugh. Everything in just 18 short months.

I didn't see her for much of it. But if I did, I obviously didn't remember. I heard somewhere we don't start forming memories until we're around 2 years old and implicit memories—those unconscious memories that stick with us automatically—aren't even until we're 7.

So essentially my mother was already dead for 3 years before I could even unconsciously think of the word "Mom" and go to her face. A face that was stolen from me. A face that I'll never see.

I'm giving you this background information now because it's vital that you understand my mom before we get into the thick of it.

I can't sit here and tell you I loved my mom unconditionally. I didn't know her. Dad was never in the picture, so grandparents were where I was shipped off to. Good people, kind people. They raised me on stories of my mom and made sure to do the one thing she'd requested when her sickness finally got her:

"Show Nick the milestone tapes."

For those unaware, a milestone tape is something a loved one, usually a parent, records a loving video to congratulate their kin on a moment they're missing out on. First day of school, marriage… you get the picture.

I remember being 5 years old, I'd not long tripped on the stairs after miscalculating my steps and smashed my front tooth on the top step, sending my first baby tooth flying. Thankfully, the pain was short-lived in my mind. I was mere days from my birthday and a surprise trip to Disneyland was coming up. In the middle of packing, I was sat down in front of the TV with my Grandpa Mihail and him putting in these pristine discs, a gaudy logo flashing up on the screen still burned into my retinas to this day:

"Gone, but not deleted: A video message from Leanora Stankowski."

The image would flicker for just a moment, always just a moment each time. Then she'd appear.

A young woman sat in a black leather armchair with a small table to her side and patterned wallpaper behind her. She was in her late 20s with her raven black hair tied in a messy bun, strands curled and dangling down her porcelain face, a beauty mark sitting just beneath her right eye, the pair of them shining like emeralds that caught the first ray of sunshine, black lipstick gave way to shimmering teeth and a smile that made even an oblivious little me feel… lost.

"Hi pumpkin, it's mommy! I hope my little prince is watching the throne while I'm away… how can you be nearly six years old and already losing your baby teeth? You're growing up too fast, little man!"

She puffed out her cheeks as she feigned a frown before giggling. My heart sank in my chest, I knew something wasn't right even then. Her tone was playful, buoyant, and full of joy, like she'd never missed a moment of my life.

"Make sure you put your tooth under your pillow tonight, Deda Mihail will make sure the tooth fairy comes and nothing else!" She raised a single finger with a wink, posing for a moment before her face fell, her posture sank and she fell back into the armchair a tad, growing smaller as she coughed. After a moment, she cleared her throat with a quiet dignity and made sure the hand she coughed into went out of shot as she fixated on the camera with a weak smile.

"Mommy loves you, my little crown prince. Close your eyes and breathe with me…"

I looked at my grandfather and, with tears streaming down his face and a bite on his lip, he put a hand on my shoulder and nodded. I did as I was told and took a long breath in, the air cold and filling my lungs, intoxicating me as I heard her words. The same words I'd come to hear at the end of every video she recorded: "I'll always be with you."

***

And so it went. For every milestone I undertook, there was an accompanying video. When I graduated middle school, when I rode my first bike… even when I broke my first bone, she had a video ready.

I was around 11, when biking home from school, I collided with a speeding driver. The bastard didn't even stop as my small body careened over his windscreen, rolled over the hood and smashed into the concrete, tearing my right arm to pieces.

Passers-by said it was a freak accident, that the car just appeared out of nowhere and then vanished. But hell, what do hit and run drivers do? Speed, speed, speed.

Medicated up to my eyes and sitting up in hospital, Grandpa handed me a mini-DVD player and the familiar face shot up. I could never tell you in those earlier videos if these were done back-to-back or months apart, but Mom still looked radiant… albeit with more coughing in each iteration.

"Hi pumpkin, it's mommy! Though, I'm sure by now you're probably cringing at the mere mention of me referring to myself that way… oh god, do people still say cringe? It's hard to know what the world you're in is like anymore, but moms are never supposed to be cool, are they?" She chuckled, a faraway look in her eye as the pit of my stomach expanded.

"No…" I thought, tears in my eyes, gripping the sheets with my good hand. "I WANT you to say those things. I WANT you to embarrass me…"

"Well, if you're watching this, then you've broken your first bone… I hope it's a bit later in life and not when you're so upset you can't even hear me. But sweetie, this is an important life lesson that I wanted to be there for: pain happens. It's a part of our world, and everyone in it must experience it. Sometimes it's physical, like now when your body hurts so much that you wanna yell and cry out. Sometimes it's emotional, which you get when someone upsets you, hurts your feelings… something you might also feel from seeing my face right now, which I'm sorry for." She trailed off, that weak smile plastered across her face like the greatest lie ever told. She took a breath, and I heard the quivers in her voice. Both from sadness and from sickness. "*But* you are my little crown prince, and while you're watching the throne, I know you'll do great things and overcome *anything* that stands in your way. You know why?"

"Why…" I breathed, my body radiating with hot pain but my heart aching. I leaned in as she leaned in, like sharing a secret only we would ever know.

"Because you're my son and my love for you will push you to do *anything*." She whispered, my face involuntarily growing into a smile without even realizing.

"Just don't look at the wall behind me."

My eyes were fixed on hers, a small sliver of the background visible behind her ear. As my eyes slowly broke from her gaze and travelled over, she spoke again.

"*Don't*." A frantic whisper escaped her lips. My eyes snapped back as a pale shade shifted out of sight.

Blinking once, I saw she was sitting back in the chair, talking as if nothing had happened. Had I dozed off? I was on high pain medication, it wasn't impossible…

"I'm running out of time. These are only supposed to be short, so I'll finish up here. Mommy loves you, my little crown prince! Close your eyes and breathe with me…"

Again, I did as instructed and heard a distinct creaking sound from the speakers, undoubtedly her settling into her chair.

"I'll always be with you."

***

So the years went, fewer milestone videos popped up. Some of them were simply mundane or not that noteworthy. Not why we're here. But the usual events: first day as a freshman, last day as a senior, prom night and even an embarrassing one wherein a 17-

year-old me had the most uncomfortable 15 minutes of being explained dating etiquette and safe sex by my long-gone mother.

By the time I'd reached 21, only four tapes remained. Grandpa Mihail had passed, and Grandma Suza was getting on, so they were given to me with the obvious instruction to not watch them until the time was right.

And this is the part where things take a turn.

A bad breakup, bad life choices, even worse friendship choices with substances readily available, a lifetime of insecurities stemming from no parental figures (all the love in the world to my grandparents, but it's not the same) and a series of videos from your long-dead mom are enough to fuck anyone up.

So, I grabbed a bottle, some pills and put the next video in, planning to binge them before I took my leave. I mean, fuck it, what's the harm if I'm ending it all, right?

The video flickered and cast a long shadow across my dismal apartment before the visage of my mom came into focus.

It'd been a couple of years since the last video and in my emotionally unstable, drunken state… I was not prepared for what I saw.

Emaciated, sunken eyes and a slack jaw, her tongue hanging out and drooping to the bottom of her chin, thick pungent saliva with her concave chest heaving under the weight of the oxygen machine wrapped around her face. A looming shadow with two bright blue orbs for eyes and jagged pillars for teeth, wrapping its arms around her.

It locked eyes with me and cocked its head to the side.

"*New.*" It croaked, my skin bubbling with fear and chilling my blood. I had never felt a terror like it.

It felt like it knew me and saw *into* me.

I recoiled and in my cocktail of fear and horror, retched up everything I'd downed not 10 minutes earlier. A torrid mixture of bile, acid, pills, and booze spread over my carpet as tears ran down my face. My stomach ached, and every cell in my body screamed at me in protest. The thoughts swirling in my thick skull were that of disappointment, disgust, and repulsiveness. I felt weak, alone and broken as I collapsed onto the floor in the foetal position, sobbing.

"Sweetie, it's Mom."

Through blurred eyes and a haze of pain I looked at the TV, half expecting some emaciated creature to lurch through, but there was my mom. She looked tired, her hair now matted to her head and exhaustion racking her bones, but beauty radiating through her as she held her hands in her lap and leaned forward, smiling.

"If you're watching this… then things are bad. I don't know how bad, but I can guess. Grandpa wouldn't have let you watch this if you'd gotten your heart broken or were at that age where emotions are as high as a kite and just as volatile… so I can assume that, much like me, you're in a bad place…" She coughed and I felt the need to sit up and give her my full attention, this woman no more than 6 years my senior frozen in time still finding ways to command my attention with her every word.

It was like I was 5 again.

"Sweetie, I know I can't talk to you like a child anymore, so I won't. Honestly, I'd been so excited to see you grow up, go through that phase where we bicker and argue over small things before finally settling in the longest and most beautiful phase of our family dynamic…" I watched her lips quiver and eyes glaze over, my own mirroring as she shakily concluded "The one where we're best friends who always look out for each other."

That broke me. Every emotion I'd trained myself to hide away when kids started asking questions I couldn't answer, situations I'd wanted my mom in, moments I felt alone… I let it out in one volatile evening of self-healing, the words on that tape echoing in my head long after it stopped playing.

"The road ahead will be tough without me. It was always going to be. But you're the crown prince and you'll eventually have that throne. Survey your kingdom and know you can do *anything* and conquer *anything*… it's getting closer now, but we still have some time left. So don't let whatever is going on beat you, nor the thing after that. The Penguins didn't, did they? I'm sure Grandpa told you, but they're my favourite… those little birds share the burden of parenthood, walk over 100 miles, and nearly starve to cultivate new life… I'd do all of that and more for you, honey. Because…"

She closed her eyes, and I did too. Without prompting, we said it together.

"I'll always be with you."

*** 

It took time to get better. All things do. I would spend so many nights in withdrawal with the shakes, vomit, and staring up at a horrific beast looming over my bed. Like the thing on the tv but foggier, it'd imitate my movements and try to get closer. With every step, its eyes would glow just a bit brighter, everything else remaining shrouded in darkness, even if light passed through my curtains.

I don't know how I made it through that time of my life.

One night, as it made its way to the foot of my bed, I closed my eyes and breathed on instinct, reciting my mother's mantra. I suppose in moments of crisis we turn to our most personal coping mechanisms, and I wasn't about to go back to the bottle. When I finished, it was gone.

Over the years, I completed my program, got clean and went through therapy to cope with the grief. When I hit 26, I met the 2nd most important woman in my life, Natalie. She knew what it was like to go through pain, to go through suffering alone. To play with the wrong demons.

We fell in love. We got engaged and eventually married. As she had been countless times before, mom was there to congratulate us.

Natalie had seen some tapes, but this was her first one that, in its own way, was directed to her. Mom was nearing the end by this point, her thin frame barely clinging to her always beautiful dresses and her skin beginning to stretch like paper. She took great gulps of air from the oxygen tank before talking, but somehow retained that exuberance she'd always had.

"I knew you'd find someone wonderful eventually, Nick. Penguins always find their mate for life, and you'd be no exception!" She giggled through strained coughs, turning her head slightly as if she could see Natalie. "I don't know you, but I bet you're the most beautiful woman in the world if my crown prince chose you. Well, after me, of course!" Another laugh, this time accompanied by tears from the two of us. "There's just one more to go… So, look after each other. Love well and experience everything you can. And don't forget…"

Natalie gripped my hand with her left, a hand on her bump with the right as we closed our eyes. I could hear the scratching sound more prominently now, but I kept my eyes shut, not wanting to ruin the moment.

"I'll always be with you."

***

We were so excited to have a baby. Natalie had come from a big family and was eager to start expanding our own. Even though I was reluctant, I couldn't help but share in her enthusiasm when so many late nights were spent fawning over baby names, cute outfits, and lofty plans for the future on how our kid would even behave around us. Determined to be "cool parents".

But in between all of that, my mind would cast back to those tapes of my mom, the only parent I really knew. I wanted to use them as a guidebook for my own steps. She'd been such an integral part of life, it seemed… odd to not have her in it now.

Keeping the last tape separate, I re-watched the entire set one by one, reliving those moments I couldn't truly appreciate until my own burgeoning journey into parenthood.

But when I got to the broken bone tape, I froze.

Once again, she leaned into the camera and whispered, eyes full of fright and panic.

"Don't look."

I pushed pause on the video and took a moment. Surely, I was just highly medicated at the time, there couldn't *really* be anything there, right?

So why was I so reluctant to move my eyes to the right to find out?

Taking a breath, I moved the video frame by frame and watched the corner where her face didn't cover.

That shadow. That same fucking shadow. Looming in the background, eyes burning red with fury.

*"Don't look. Don't look. Don't look. Don't look."*

I jumped, the video was skipping, stuck on the sounds of my mother's panic-stricken voice begging me not to stare, but I couldn't help it. I stared and watched this creature take confident, unnatural, and twitchy strides from the background, getting ever closer to the camera. I saw the muscles on its face twist and undulate as it pressed its cheeks up into a twisted grin, the sight of rot and earth and unspeakable things in its mouth all displaying themselves in full glory as it intonated one word that sent screams through my home before shutting off.

"*Soon.*"

*******

Natalie was 8 months gone, petite and a history of prior drug abuse. They said her heart just couldn't take it, her body gave out, and that it was a miracle our daughter survived.

I took it all in and yet none of it as I cradled my entire universe in my arms, the second greatest woman I'd ever known now taken from me too.

"Phoebe." I breathed, unable to take my eyes off of her perfect little face as she slept soundly just 12ft from her dead mother. "Her name is Phoebe, and she is the crown princess."

Somewhere in the corner of my eye, a shadow cast itself over Natalie's bed, right as they put the sheet over her.

From that night on, there would always be noises outside our home. Always faint howling. Always a solitary spot in the front of the property where no light could touch it.

For a while, I forgot about the videos. Forgot about everything that wasn't Phoebe. Raising her became priority #1 and I would work any extra hours I needed to, give up any friendship I had to and spite myself in whatever way was necessary to ensure that my perfect girl slept soundly at night.

It wasn't until Phoebe's 2nd birthday last week that I finally got the courage to dig out the videos and watch the last one.

How many times had I sat in a home, emotionally destroyed and at a crossroads in my life, waiting to see this woman's face and hope she'd somehow have the magic words to guide me?

As the picture flickered on, the logo shining up on screen. I cast my head back with a mixture of surprise and sadness as I realised the significance of the year: I was older than her now.

"Hi sweetie, I guess we've finally reached the end, huh?"

Her voice sounded... younger. I looked down and saw her standing up. No chair or wallpaper in sight. It looked like she was recording this in her bedroom, a picture of health, all things considered. Her eyes red from crying but her voice unwavering, like she'd prepared these words carefully.

"This is technically the final video for you, but the first for me. Weird how this all works, but this is how it needs to happen...

if you're watching this, you've got your own little princess to protect. The crown prince has now become the king, and I couldn't be prouder!" She beamed, but my stomach tightened at those words.

"Your own little princess."

I breathed, my chest tightening. How did she know?

"I imagine you're now wondering how I know. Well, that's not the important part. What's important is if you saw what you think you saw. Within the videos, between the frames. There is something lurking here, Nick. Something ancient."

I felt the house shudder, settling into place, no doubt. But I couldn't separate myself from the fear running through my body.

"It feeds on misfortune. It watches from the shadows and waits for small, tiny windows to make itself known. I don't know where it came from or what it is, but I know what it wants…"

A rumbling behind me, the sound of wood splintering and creaking. The unmistakable sound of tapping that I'd heard every time we did the mantra at the end of a video. I was shaking, but I didn't stop watching.

"It wants us, Nick. We seem to be a… source for it. When it finishes using us, it moves on. A long time ago… I was told that if I captured it in film, solidified it in these repeatable tapes, it would slow it down… maybe even stop it. I have no idea if it'll work, but you deserve to know now that you can almost certainly see it too. Because if it doesn't stop here, if *you* start to see it… start to experience misfortune…"

My heart skipped. Tripping over the stairs and narrowly missing cracking my skull as a child, losing my first tooth. The hit and run that shattered my arm, my first broken bone. Marrying and losing Natalie, my first love…

Oh no.

Oh god, no.

I willed my body to move, to leap out of the seat and rush to Phoebe's room, but I had to hear the rest through, screaming at my mom to tell me the solution.

"When your Deda Mihail told me about our curse… how he took me in after my father died… about how it passes from father to daughter, mother to son, and so forth… You can try to avoid it, but it always finds a way…" She looked down in shame, clutching at her sleeves. "Truth be told, I didn't want to get pregnant. But things have a way of happening and I knew I couldn't give you up." She glanced behind her, something off camera scaring her into grabbing at her arms and rubbing them, shame and fear on her face. "I'm so sorry, baby. But I want you to know that there is power in these words. In these videos. I will do *everything* I can to protect you, just like I know you'll protect your child. No matter who it hurts in the process. Because…"

One last time. I just had to close my eyes one last time and it would all be over.

I did it on instinct. It didn't matter that there was a slew of sounds alerting me to an invading presence in my home. That it was rapidly approaching me.

All that mattered was the mantra.

*"I'll be here for you, always."*

But what I heard parroting me back was not my mother.

A guttural, inhuman voice barked back the phrase and I swear I felt its breath inches from my face. I felt eyes unrestricted by pupils or sockets spin around, focusing on my weakest point. But I didn't waver.

After a few agonising moments, it darted away and out of view, leaving only the static of the TV to keep me aware that I wasn't in fact dreaming.

As soon as I knew it was safe, I ran to Phoebe's room and checked on her, convinced that she was next in a long line of losses. Convinced that some otherworldly spectre had taken her from me.

Convinced I would be alone again.

You can imagine my relief when I opened the door to find her softly sleeping, clutching her teddy bear with his own attached blankie. The same toy my mom had given me.

I looked at her with the enormity of the situation overshadowing me. The realisation she was the same age I was when my mom got diagnosed.

The realisation that soon, I would be the one making a slew of videos for milestones I'd never get to see her inherit.

My crown princesses' kingdom of nightmares.

And I don't know if this is what my mother intended, but I took those words at the end to heart.

"Protect your child. No matter who it hurts in the process."

*******

I'm sorry, everyone.

I don't know *how* this translates across mediums, but there is power in describing an old and malevolent force. Just like there is seeing it in the corner of your eye or when you experience a lucky break from death. A misstep here and a wrong turn there. You'll always see it.

My mother gave up everything to buy time, give me the chance to right the wrongs and find a better way, a way that involves my daughter growing up with her father in her life, without the plague of whatever this is hanging over either of us.

Maybe you won't be the one, maybe it will simply look at you and find you not to its liking as it did me that fateful night, inches away from my flesh and determining that I simply wasn't "ripe enough" yet.

But someone will come across this, and it will bite. It will bite and never let go. Be it nightmares, sleep paralysis, a slew of unfortunate mishaps or something flitting in the corner of your eye, it'll be there. Whatever it is.

Waiting.

I wish you well, and I hope you don't judge me too harshly.

But to me and to Phoebe, family is everything.

So, close your eyes and take a deep breath.

*Because they'll always be with you.*

# THE SIRENS CAVE

"I heard that Cave Mitrione has another name, The Sirens Cave. Folks say there's a gust that flows through the cave and causes the sounds of people calling to you."

"I heard it ain't just the wind, some old settlers and explorers got stuck down there. Shit got real and before they knew it... boom, they were gone. Maybe they fell into the pit?"

My two friends, Trey and Anthony, kept on discussing the majesties of this strange cave in the middle of nowhere outside of our town. Some 70 miles north, there was a large swathe of land housing a large cave that held the eponymous Wailing Cave. I was always up for adventure, being 17 and spending most of my life outdoors, but it was the insistence of my two aforementioned friends and their propensity to do far more daring feats that lead us to this particular adventure.

"C'mon, Bryce, you know if we TELL our folks, they'll just stop us. Or, worse yet, insist on coming with and providing boring rules we don't need." Trey jabbed my shoulder playfully. "We're strong, virile men! We don't need any of that shit. Plus, we're not going to need much more than ropes, lights, backpack, and some basic gear. We'll be in and out with either a boring story to tell, or..."

"Or footage that will net us those huuuuge YouTube bucks. Yeah, Trey, I know." I rolled my eyes, imitating his enthusiasm. "Alright, I'm in. What are we doing?"

Anthony stood up from my bed, hands on his back, looking over at the map. He was very much the brains of the operation.

"Alright, we'll leave at 5am tomorrow. Bryce, borrow your sister's car and pick us up. If your mom asks, tell her we're going hiking or something, don't say the cave... obviously. If you're super worried about location tracking and your mom not believing you, turn it off. We'll get to the cave before sunrise and be back home by early morning. If anyone asks, we were just doing some bonding in the mountains. Kay?"

"Bonding in the mountains? Won't that make people think…" Trey started before Anthony let out an audible sigh and we broke into laughter. "Hey, it's cool, bro, no judging here. I mean, I *know* I'm your type, but my girlfriend may have questions…"

After some light arguing and insistence by Anthony that wasn't what he meant, we broke open some beers to celebrate the plans in motion and got an early night.

When I slept, I envisioned a small opening in the side of a large cliff edge… no bigger than me and almost as if it were manufactured to my size and stature. I felt my body drawn to it and even when I tried to resist, my limbs were inescapably pulled into the perfectly shaped holes in the wall.

Slipping into the wall, I felt the constricting nature of bedrock push on my muscles, squeezing at my bones and ripping at my flesh as I pushed even further in. I could hear someone… something calling out to me from the depths.

Then, in an instant, my body was wrenched forward at an astounding rate. My skin split and I felt burning all over as I screamed for the dream to stop.

When I awoke, I was lying in a cold sweat and staring down at the bedroom floor, my covers wrapped all around me like a boa constrictor.

What the fuck was that?

***

We set about making our preparations in the morning. I felt the cold chill of November air hit my skin as I went downstairs and grabbed my gear from the garage and thanked my sister for the car… even if it meant bribing her 50 bucks to not tell mom where we were going.

By the time I picked up the guys and we'd reached the cave, it was nearly 6 am, dawn was still some time away, but it wouldn't be long before the sunlight exposed our early hour abseiling, and we were pretty confident this place was state property. None of us wanted to get caught by state troopers or the police for trespassing.

We worked quickly to get our gear and head down to the mouth of the cave.

This thing was gigantic. Built into the side of a great rocky mountain that stretched across the surrounding planes, connecting at the base to a slew of other jagged giants that rose into the sky and looked as if they'd puncture the very clouds. The cave's depths were unknown to us, but the width of the mouth gave us a decent inkling, over 70ft wide and 30ft high gave us all the foreboding we needed.

"Damn… big mouth, huh?" Trey remarked, trying to find a joke that fit within his addled, juvenile mind. "Guess she can take all 3 of us at once, eh?"

Nervous laughter filled the awkward silence as neither I nor Anthony wanted to be the first to venture in. We had very little light beyond the first few feet and didn't expect to turn on our headlamps so early. Nevertheless, we ventured forth together and within a few minutes, the entrance's warmth gave way to cold indifference inside the cave.

The entrance was simple. It jutted down on a slightly steep incline for around 5 minutes before widening into a fork that split two ways: one going left and up, the other going right and down. Pausing for a moment to listen for any distinct sounds, we heard something emanate from the right path.

A soft, guttural wailing.

"You think it's…" I began, eyeing the passageway with anticipation and concern, Trey rubbing his hands together.

"Oh, hell yeah, I think it's the pit! We ready?" Before we even replied, he set off ahead and left me and Anthony still faced with the foreboding nature of venturing on.

We both knew there was something unseemly.

"What did you say this cave was called? Sirens Call? I'd not heard that one before." I remarked, carefully trudging forth to catch up with Trey and flinching at every small juddering of the cave walls. Anthony scoffed and picked up his pace.

"Clues in the name, bud. The Sirens Call was the original moniker locals gave this place, said it housed something deep in the pit that fed off of those with weak wills. Used the voices of those they loved to entice them in and devour them. Natives said it was an evil spirit and told the authorities to seal the cave off, but of course they never did. It became The Wailing Cave sometime later to help with tourism and I can't say I blame 'em. It sure as hell brought US here."

"Yeah, illegally, might I add," I remarked, forcing a smile. "Still though, creepy as fuck name…"

We nodded and turned the final corner into a large opening, the ceiling of the cave hundreds of feet above us, a pair of tunnels on the other side of the clearing around 200ft across from us. In the centre sat a pit with raised bricks around the opening, the width of it easily 100ft.

Even coming close to it brought me anxiety, but not as much as seeing Trey securing his line to the side of the pit and giving us a thumbs up as he abseiled down.

"See you fuckers soon, I'm gonna get us some monayyy!" He called as he descended into the darkness. We shook our heads and tried to contain our concerns. Trey was always the daredevil among us. He'd once broken his leg trying to evade law enforcement, scaling a large fence, and not even thinking about the drop afterwards.

But when the line grew taught and the snapping sound bounced around the cave, we knew something was wrong.

"Trey? TREY!" I called out, no response.

We ran over and peered down the pit, his line still attached and absolute darkness after the first 10ft. We held onto the line and tried pulling against it in vain, worried he'd passed out from hitting his head. A sense of absolute dread filled my body the longer I stared, Anthony's forehead breaking out in a cold sweat as we waited for a response.

We got it. In the form of the line snapping and Trey's terrified screams as he fell further and further down.

It was a horrific, visceral sound that sent my knees buckling and Anthony grabbing me to stop my momentum dragging me into the pit with him.

"We NEED to go. We have to get help. NOW." He cried, shaking my shoulders until I saw sense. I nodded, and we dashed for the entrance.

What followed chilled my blood and stopped us dead in our tracks.

"Hey, HEY! I'm fine, I'm fine. Just spooked the shit outta me is all, don't panic. Jeeze. Just come back and throw me a line, I'll be able to get up!"

Anthony breathed a sigh of relief and began walking back. But I pulled on his collar and shook my head, eyes wide and full of fear, a finger up to my lips.

"Wh-what? He's stuck down there, dude! We gotta help him!" He hissed, keeping his voice low as I asked.

"Did you hear his body hit the ground?" I asked, his eyes fixated on mine and not responding when I asked. "Did you HEAR his body hit the ground, Anthony?"

He swallowed, looked over his shoulder and back at me, shaking his head.

"How deep is that pit? If you were to guess?" I pressed him, a transference of nerves between us as we kept quiet.

"Guys? Ya still there? I can just about make out your voices, come and help me, man! We ain't gonna get that sweet YouTube Stack with me staying down here!" He called, concern and fear wracking his voice.

"I'd… I'd say over 500 feet, if not deeper." He replied, the fear mounting the more he spoke. "So, if he did fall with the length of the rope, bringing him down maybe 200 feet…"

"He'd be dead. He didn't use anywhere near enough to scale that far down. So…" I let the question linger in the air for a moment as a chill ran through the cave. Was it the breeze the natives mentioned?

"So, what is calling out to us from the pit?" He finally intonated, our foreboding growing like a cancer as we stared at the pit just 30 feet away.

"Trey, what is your girlfriend's birthday?" I called out, an idea popping to mind.

"Huh? Why? Guys, this ain't 21 questions. Come over and help me, I feel fine but that may be adrenaline. I need a life outta here, now c'mon!" He shouted back, Anthony taking another step forward.

"Answer the question, Trey. We just wanna make sure all is fine. You know the legend of this cave as well as we do. How far down are you?" He called out, the frustration apparent now in Trey's voice.

"For fuck's sake… It's sometime in April, I can't remember when, okay? And I'd say I fell maybe 50 feet? It's soft down here, I guess it broke my fall. Happy?!"

Anthony and I exchanged looks as he shook his head, backing away towards me.

"I hear you walking away… damnit, Anthony! Hey! You're the smartest guy I know, so I got a question for you: if you're THAT worried I'm not who I say I am… which, if you'll pardon the expression, is fucking STUPID… who am I?" I swear his voice shifted just a tad as he asked that last question, but he didn't stop. "You've always been the sorta guy who LOVED mysteries. Imagine what secrets are down here, what you could know if you saw what I see. All you have to do… is throw me a line. I'll tell you everything."

Anthony's eyes were wide, darting between me and him. I couldn't understand how this was even a difficult choice. It clearly wasn't Trey or, if it was, he was not someone we could save on our own with our limited equipment. Why was this so hard for him?

But seeing that glazed look in his eyes, the slackness of the jaw as he walked over to the pit and threw a line, I realised why the cave used to be called "The Sirens Call".

"I'm begging you, Anthony, come with me. We can save Trey within a couple of hours with the right people. We don't need to put ourselves at risk." I reached out a hand, not willing to get close but also worried about my friend's slowly deteriorating sanity.

He looked at the rope and looked at me, holding out a hand, keeping his dominant one on the line of rope as it fell down and knocked against the inner pit wall.

In an instant, it grew taut and snapped as Anthony was pulled into the pit headfirst. His screaming filled the cave and threatened to burst my eardrums with their piercing shrill. I turned away and covered my head until it stopped reverberating.

As silence greeted me, I felt my body surge with adrenaline and all things urged me to go to the entrance.

But, as Anthony's calm voice called from the pit, a malaise overcame me and while I didn't dare turn around, I suddenly felt it difficult to make any sudden moves.

"Bryce, you were always a loyal friend. The furniture in the room that tied us together. You're never going to make it outside without us. You know that."

"I gotta agree with Ant, you're sorta like the yes man but awkward, full of self-doubt and undesirable traits. Ain't nobody gonna want that complex mess."

I felt tears fill my eyes and rush down my cheeks. Something was crawling out of the pit, scaling its walls with thick digits digging into the rock and grunting as it ascended.

"I can't join you. I have a life out there and so do you… so do my friends that you're using to talk right now!" I clenched my fists, trying to move but still unable. "Why can't you let them go? Why can't you let us all go?!"

Something pulled at the outside of the pit, scratching against the mortar and panting. It sounded large.

"Then how else would we talk to you? We have no voice of our own, we know no other way than to be used as meat puppets." It gurgled and laughed as Anthony spoke, his voice breaking down and distorting.

Whatever was behind me was finding its way to me, and the voice grew closer. It was so visceral and real that I almost turned around.

"Good joke, Trey. After all, we're all meat puppets in the end. SO why wait? Besides…"

Hot breath pushed against my ankles. It was so close.

"You smell ready to us."

At that moment, my fear gave way to flight, and I bolted for the passage, dropping my back on whatever was behind me. It contained several pieces of heavy equipment that I had prepped for my own abseiling and that being unceremoniously brought down on ANYONE would hurt. The thing howled as my pace picked up.

"So ready. Why Wait? SO Ready. WHY WAIT?" It bellowed, claws and hot breath tearing into the walls as I rushed, my eyes blurring and body aching as I pushed through the agony.

As soon as light filled the opening, the panting stopped. No cry of pain or slinking into the darkness, it simply ceased. I didn't dare turn around until I was back at the top of the hill leading to the mouth.

When I did, I saw nothing.

Simply the entrance to a cave none of us should have ever ventured into.

With my friends still trapped inside.

***

The drive home was filled with anxiety, fear and pain. I did the right thing and contacted the state police on my way back. They mounted a search and declared that Anthony and Trey's deaths were entirely by accident. Death by misadventure was the official cause of death. We were called stupid boys looking for a thrill, and the town by and large felt sympathetic to me.

Life moved on and even several years later, still living in that small rocky town, I get looks of sympathy and pity.

"Poor boy, he still thinks there's something there. Can't accept being the only one, I suppose…" They'd say, looking at me as if I were a lost lamb with no idea of where to go or what to do. Even my own family gave me a wide berth, therapy, and support.

But I knew better, I still do now.

The Cave has been closed off properly for some time. Nobody is smart enough to venture close since the incident. But that doesn't stop people trying, curious to see if the legends of Cave Mitrione, The Wailing Cave, The Sirens Call are as grizzly and blood curdling as they heard.

But… at least I hope they'll never learn the truth.

Not long after the incident, I had those nightmares again, enticing me into my own private little hole in the wall. Squeezing and constricting me.

Only now, I saw my friends at the end of this increasingly claustrophobic tunnel, calling to me in pain to join them, to help them.

I sought out a native man in the area and told him of what happened. He listened and never judged or thought of me as a fool.

Instead, his face grew full of sorrow, and he handed me a totem to keep with me.

"Spirits inhabit that cave, the kind that can never truly rest. They will always wish to pull more in and add to their energy. You were most likely their target from your dreams, the others simply used as bait."

Some nights, I don't just awaken in a cold sweat from the nightmares.

Some nights, I find myself standing at the front of my window, staring in the direction of the cave, now seemingly visible from so far a distance, beckoning me. When I drive through the mountains for work, I hear them. I hear them so clearly.

I hear their voices as clear as I hear my own families calling into my ear: "So ready. Why Wait?"

# HEADLIGHTS ON/HEADLIGHTS OFF

They say this trail covers ancient land. That the things you find along here aren't for the normal minded to see.

Honestly, I just took a detour after a rough night and decided that this was a good excuse to lengthen out my drive and listen to some good music, but now I'm dictating my thoughts to my notepad like a neurotic asshole because a stream of consciousness spoken to nobody seems too weird to me. I'd rather be Dale Cooper than Jack Torrance.

The in-car system still lets dulcet tones from my Lo-Fi playlist hang in the air, the wonders of modern technology, I suppose. Not so loud that it drowns out my thoughts or interrupts the beauty of the drive, but enough to allow me to be introspective and feel like I'm going on my own trip of self-discovery.

Right, the trip, of course…

The first thing you see as you come off the last turning on the finely paved concrete is a series of signs that lead off onto a dirt road that stretches into the darkness and dips out of sight.

The first was the normal highway sign, standing at the back with a slight crook to the side, the paint flaking away at the edges, but the sign shimmering in front of my car's lights:

*"A705 (N)*

*A705 (S)*

*M. Road, 300yards west."*

There was a crude sign hanging in front, practically peering down at me from a clearly damaged pole in the dirt, the letters scratched and blotchy.

"Stretching out in front of you is a featured oddity within U. B. Dedra's Dusklight Circus… The transfixing allure of The Myopic Road beckons all! Simply start your journey and let the delights find you." A small post-it note had been attached to the bottom, hastily scribbled:

*"Remember: Do NOT turn on your headlights. Do not expose the trail ahead. Drive slow and drive safe!"*

It's the dead of night. This part of the country doesn't have many folks out to these back roads at the best of times and quarantine simply exacerbated that. I took a deep breath and looked at my knuckles as they gripped the steering wheel. Skin tearing away and raw flesh exposed, stinging in the wake of the biting cold.

I thought of what I had driven away from. What I'm always trying to get away from.

I close my eyes and see the looming red shapes, the haze of anger and the hot flush of pain. I grip the steering wheel tighter and clench my teeth as I put my foot down and turn the wheel towards the road.

The Myopic Road is simply an unofficial title, of course. No planning committee would sign off on such a strange name. Not even a very subtle one, for that matter. Short sighted because of the sheer darkness enveloping the trail from side to side inevitably causing accidents... our ancestors have a very ugly sense of humour.

But it was fitting. The road was something of an anomaly in my hometown and while nobody had been actively dissuaded from going down it, nobody ever needed to reinforce the fear we all felt.

No, the accidents were a frequent enough reminder.

If you drove down the road with respect and patience, they say it's just a good place to cleanse the mind and help you focus. Plenty have come out the other side without problems, or so they say.

But there were many... FAR too many who didn't obey the rules, didn't heed them, or even see them.

Be it someone intoxicated behind the wheel, those escaping the law, joyriders, or just general thrill seekers, they all would inexplicably find themselves coming down The Myopic Road and they would almost always find themselves meeting with an ugly end.

Sometimes, patrol cars would find the wreckage after a couple of days, scraps of their clothing and maybe even an identifiable piece of the person. Other times, a single liver could find itself draped over the sign leading into the trail 10 years after its owner went missing.

But often times most people didn't get found at all. No vehicle, no trace.

When police officers would pursue offenders towards this trail, they'd simply stop at the threshold and flash their headlights, desperately trying to convince them to come back, that any fate is better than what lay down that road.

Or maybe they were hoping, wishing in vain, that the driver had seen the one rule when traversing down the myopic road:

**DO NOT TURN ON YOUR HEADLIGHTS.**

So, here I am. I've been driving for about 10 minutes now at a relatively slow pace. The moonlight above has helped me see just a bit ahead, and I can feel my mind wandering. I remember the last thing I said out loud to a living, breathing person.

*"How dare you... I'm not standing for this bullshit anymore, you hear me? I hope you fucking choke!"*

I remember the hot bile in my throat and my shaking fists as I spat venom in their face, their eyes wide and full of fear and rage. I remember my fist connecting with their jaw over and over before I finally—

What the fuck?

I had to stop…

There's something in the road.

The clearing is narrowing, these huge trees permeate every aspect of my windscreen and tower over me. They're old and some are gnarled, the bark is blackened and small insects crawl over them. I think I see birds perched on a pair of branches just above me, but I can't recall ever seeing birds with necks that long or eyes that white…

The moon's light is beginning to wane and the further I traverse, the harder it is to make things out, but it didn't stop me seeing the thing some 20ft ahead of me. Hunched over as if vomiting, shoulders rotating and shuddering as the hind legs read up.

My hand instinctively goes for the little dial that turns on my headlights, and I stop myself.

*"Do not turn on the headlights."*

Fuck…

I take a look back and try to figure out if I can reverse on the trail, do a 3-point turn and go back.

But by now, it's obvious that the embankment on either side is high and the trees are too close to allow for space.

Fuck.

Nothing else for it, I tell myself. I push down on the pedal and move forward slowly, revving the engine in hopes that this deer-like creature gets the hint and scarpers.

It doesn't.

I see its hind legs rise off the ground and twist towards me, a single bulbous eye fixing on me.

I honk the horn on instinct and this thing immediately drops down to all fours and runs off for the woods.

I've been driving again now for a few minutes; the road is getting darker but I'm doing as instructed and letting my mind wander. Every kick, shove, punch, and barbed jab brings me a new wave of renewed anger and disgust. That filthy pig thinking they could EVER make things right, that it was "just a one off", promising "Never again". Pathetic. I can still feel my clenched fists gleefully smashing into their face over and over, the crunching of their nose and the tears in their eyes as they begged and pleaded for mercy. Ha! Mercy should never be given to scum like that.

A smile curls around my lips as I feel my thighs sear with hot pain, my neck tightening and my entire frame reliving the muscle memory of fights long past. The road was beginning to dip, and I can sense a bend was coming up, not something I expected.

It's only when I take a look in my rear-view mirror on instinct that I see it.

Bloodshot eyes, black fur eclipsing all of its features save for the tusks protruding from its top lips. Viscous black liquid dripping off of them.

This thing was matching my smile and I watch its fucking pupils dilate as if it were getting ready to pounce.

I floor it without thinking and… Fuck. I made the most critical mistake.

Headlights on.

It was just for a moment, just to get me away safely from this thing and see where the fuck I was going.

But it showed me what was lurking on the sides of the trees, clinging to the branches, crawling at the depths of my peripheral vision. I saw flesh move in ways it shouldn't, human bodies devoid of features save for long, dark streaks of red. I saw too much.

I saw something I didn't wish to see. Their body, broken and battered beyond repair, laying in the road, mangled as if… as if they'd been run over by…

They looked up at me for just a moment.

No.

**Headlights off.**

I checked the locks were on the door and burst into tears. Shameful, angry tears. My knuckles hurt more than ever, and razors line my throat as I hold back a scream.

I remember grabbing my things and leaving; they were choking on the floor and begging me to stay.

I remember the fear in their words as they struggled to move broken fingers and speak between mouthfuls of blood and broken teeth.

I remember the *hatred* I felt for them when I took one last look at them and had all the power in the world, telling them the one thing I knew would haunt them forever.

*"I will go to the one place you cannot follow. You will NEVER have me."*

I heard them stumble to get up as I went for the door. A slip, a grunt, a bump, a crack, and a slump to the floor.

But I did not look back. Not once.

I don't like to think of what happened to them. Not out of fear for the repercussions, but for fear of returning to my old self that sympathised with them, that coddled to them, that DEPENDED on them.

Something moved in the trees by my window. It was gangly, small, and flung itself from the base of the trees with arms too wide for its frame, like a comic book character enshrouded in darkness.

The birds overhead are still on that same branch. They've grown in number and their necks are twisting as they look down at me. I know they're eying me up now, the drool from their beaks coating my windscreen and hissing as it makes contact.

Maybe I deserve to be here. Maybe this is my punishment for letting my temper get the better of me and inflicting pain on someone I was supposed to love.

That age old adage of "they deserved it" seems hollow in my throat even now when I dictate it. Words crumbling to dust as they pass my teeth and echo when succeeding my lips, hanging in the stale air of my car as a mocking reminder of my pure weakness.

I'll show them weakness.

I wipe my tears away and look ahead to the now barely lit road. It continues to descend and I see no signs of it levelling out, but I put my foot down and accelerate, regardless.

**Headlights on.**

The quicker I go, the more begins to reach out from the sides of the car. Sometimes, I think I recognise them in that fleeting moment. An old friend I once said something cruel to in jest, a university roommate whose food I surreptitiously ate when they had little to no money, an ex I'd cheated on… my lover. All of them momentarily highlighted by nothing more than natural lighting and waning instincts, their faces contorted into hideous expressions of rage, malnourished bodies reaching out with frail limbs as they try to get a hold of my car.

I almost don't see them in the road. I slam on my breaks and stare at them, their towering figure all the more imposing in the isolation of this road. Not a single scrap of skin left on their body, only pure red flesh. Their face full of bruises. A black eye and tears of blood running down their face as what remains of their jaw intonates the same words.

*"NEVER AGAIN."*

They take long, powerful steps towards the hood of my car.

*"NEVER AGAIN, ALONE. "*

They place two broken, mangled hands on the sides of the hood and leap forward, their broken face frozen between despair and rage as they rear their head back and careen their skull into the windscreen over and over as their pained shrieks get louder, the glass threatening to shatter as it distorts under the pressure.

Everything floods back and, in that moment, I am once again my old self and full of an incalculable fear.

But it is only when they speak aloud that full sentence do I snap out of it.

*"NEVER AGAIN, WILL YOU BE ALONE."*

**Headlights off.**

I will not be that person again.

I accelerate fast, brake hard and watch as they go flying, their body greeting the pavement with a vile crunch as they twist and crunch, coming to a stop some 15 feet ahead of me, twitching.

I feel my knuckles burn as they grip the steering wheel, and I resist the urge to get out and finish the job with my bare hands.

"Broken promises from a broken person." I spit. "You will never be anything more."

I push hard on the accelerator as the car thunders over them, offering no resistance as they slip under the tyres and two short, sickening bumps follow as I continue on.

It didn't take long for the bravado to slip, however.

10 minutes down the road, I slow to a crawl and roll the window down to vomit between sobs. The air is thick with iron, and I can hear a croaking emanating from the embankment opposite my window. It fills my head with nauseating thoughts and my eyes start to glaze over. But the jerking sensation of my engine stalling is enough to pull me back inside.

The road is levelling out now, the moon overhead casting a powerful yellow glow over the pathway, now not dissimilar to that of a super-moon… maybe even bigger. I can see the jagged cracks on its surface, thick blots and… was the moon always so split? I feel like it's pulsating when I stare at it… or is it simply getting closer?

That is not the moon.

There's a small black dot in the centre of it, following me as I start down the road, a low drone growing in volume as I pick up speed down this stretch of road, desperate for an exit. How can this go on for so long? Surely there's an end in sight…

I feel my thoughts start to spill out and dissipate before I can fully comprehend them, like my mind is a sponge being squeezed of all moisture. When I look up at the orb, I see thick red veins around the sides, splitting it.

It's an eye.

THEIR eye.

Never letting me out of their sight for a moment, as was always the way. That drone their incessant call to action, a threat of what would occur if I didn't respond in a timely fashion.

Think what you will of me, but I did what I had to do, and I am NOT sorry for it. They can follow me to the ends of the earth, but I will not apologise for taking a stand.

When you love someone, you're supposed to protect them, to make them a part of your own heart and entrust yours in kind. It is safety, trust, vulnerability and so much more.

It is never meant to be a microcosm of fear, subjugation, and pain.

I know what the road is doing, what it is showing me.

My sins, my failures, my fears.

They all go back to *them*. As they always have done.

That last night, they had followed me incessantly from room to room, not allowing me a moment's respite. And, like a shadow, they clung to me, seeping into my skin, and making it burn from the inside out. I could not breathe from the suffocation both metaphorically and, inevitably, literally when I would request space.

I don't know what triggered me to finally stand up for myself. Perhaps it was the way they'd been acting in our latest quarantine, staring at me like a predator sizing up a meal. Maybe it was the constant humming over me while I slept, as if grappling with their own instincts to kill.

But either way, I felt their thin fingers wrap around my neck and their barbed words as they spat expletive after expletive.

"You pathetic pig, nobody will EVER want you the way I do. You belong to ME, and I will do with you as I see fit. You're less than the roadkill birds feed on." They'd grin and watch as the life faded from my eyes just enough that they could let go and know I was on the verge of passing out.

I heaved as they let me go, still clawing at my throat in a desperate attempt to rid their presence of me and my soft sobs filling the room.

They didn't like that.

*"Oh my GOD I don't fucking CARE can you shut up?!"* A powerful kick met my stomach as I lay prone on the ground, their hands over their heads and genuine anger on their faces, as if I'd just spat on them. *"You don't EVER think about the consequences of your actions, do you? Did you ever consider that you wouldn't be here... WE wouldn't be here if you just didn't fuck up all the time?!"*

I remember they kneeled down, and their bright blue eyes shimmered as they gently cupped my face and flashed that smile that immediately put me under their spell, but I may as well have been face to face with a crocodile.

*"You know I could kill you and nobody would fucking care about a freak like you, right? Nobody will ever love you. Never again. You will ALWAYS be alone."*

My right hand connected with their jaw and the force was strong enough to dislocate it in one fell swoop. They collapsed back and looked at me in bewilderment, their eyes full of fear, and if anyone walked in on us at that moment, you'd think I was their lifelong tormenter.

They had no understanding of why they deserved to be punished, why they deserved pain and torment. They truly believed in their hearts that they were above such things.

And that made me angrier.

I can see the thing above growing red. The road is becoming dim, and I can sense that wide-eyed beast is gaining on the car, but I will not relent.

I will not stop.

With every successive strike, I felt them wither under my weight. They kept bleating out that same pathetic line.

*"Never again. Will always be alone."*

When they stumbled and fell, I was sure they were close to death from sound alone. Yet I refused to go back and help.

I wanted them to know true loneliness in those final moments, callous as it may be.

I must sound like such a horrible person to you, despite everything I endured. But my hands are shaking as I grip the steering wheel. The road has darkened and as I go slower, I can feel this thing gaining on me, determined to do god knows what once it catches up to me.

The road is beginning to climb now, in the dim light left I can see a steep curve going up. I will need to push on the accelerator and… oh…

There are pits across the road, numerous potholes that could easily stall the car if I'm not careful.

I cannot do it in the darkness.

Perhaps Myopic Road is not unlike the journey of self-discovery. We start our maddening descent. We face our troubles at the middling road, and we continue our road to healing and betterment with the uphill struggle.

Or maybe I'm simply terrified beyond belief and wishing to make sense of a place that is devoid of almost none.

I can't go back now, the police will have discovered the body and no matter what defence I offer, I will be trading one prison for another.

No, this road is all I have left now.

I think I will put on some music for the last leg of the journey. The red eye above is pulsating, but I think it is not dissimilar to my lover: if you fight against it and show defiance, it will hold no sway over you, even if fear grips every fibre of my being.

Perhaps I won't find anything, and I'll simply go until my car runs out of gas, letting the beasts of this wood take me.

Maybe I'll get to the other side and be a free person for the first time in my adult life.

Maybe the shape some ways up the road, towering over the trees with long antlers jutting out of its skull will be helpful, not a hindrance.

Either way, I must drive.

Whatever happens, happens.

Put yourself before anyone else. Do not let their anger and fear become a catalyst for pain and suffering. You will always have the power to take agency back and break free, hopefully in a less violent way than I did.

The Myopic Road will be waiting for you when you wish to make your own journey.

Perhaps I will be, too.

**Headlights on.**

# DID NOBODY ELSE PLAY THE BATH GAME?

Did *nobody* else play "The Bath Game"

Ok, let me just get straight to the point:

I do not believe for one second that no other child played the bath game growing up. I'm convinced my friends are trolling me, but they're not responding to my messages and so I'm left with little choice to bring my question here, hoping SOMEONE will know what the hell I'm talking about.

I was around 5 or 6 years old when my babysitter introduced the idea of The Bath Game to me. She said it was a fun way to engage the imagination and that I could find something truly special within the water.

I didn't question it, even then, because she was the boss and I thought she was pretty. I didn't wanna make her mad by refusing or risk having my Nintendo taken away if I was disobedient. So, when my mom told her to bathe me one night, I was excited to try it!

Her instructions were pretty simple, and I'd come to write them down, because with any game there HAS to be rules:

*1: You must do the bath game alone. These instructions can be given, but you have to be isolated for the game to begin.*

*2: The tub should have some sort of thick bath soap that includes a lot of suds and a dark liquid. Ensure the top of the water is obscured and the sides are caked in it, including the handles to get out.*

*3: Only hot water. No cold and no resistance upon getting into the water. If it hurts, it will pass as your skin gets used to it. Ignore any reddening on the skin.*

*4: Take a deep breath, make sure it hurts just a little, know you will not be coming back up for a while.*

*5: Dive in and don't look back or rise up. Allow the current to take you and keep your eyes open.*

*6: Your vision will blur, but it will eventually clear, and you'll see something in the plughole. Go to it.*

*7: Trust in what you see, let your body relax.*

8: When you meet the sea emperor and the lights above the water go out, you've won the bath game and can come up for air!

The babysitter was so excited she could barely contain herself, bouncing around and eyes wide, a thick liquid flowing from her eyes. She didn't even bother wiping it, content to be sharing in my submersion by proxy.

I stood there in my bath towel and expecting her to follow me in, but she shook her head, nostrils flaring.

"Only you. Rule 1, remember?" She beamed, and I felt my face grow hot. She was so pretty. When she stared at me like that I'd have done anything. "You're special, I can't wait for you to win and get your prize!"

"What do I get?" I was eager, but I HAD to know. What kid didn't love prizes?

Her lip twitched, and she took a moment to answer, but I remember her expression never changed. Not once. Her teeth chattered as she said one word:

"FREEDOM."

I had no idea what she meant, but in my mind, I assumed like any child it was gaming all night, eating what I wanted and no school… what kid wouldn't want that?

I went in and noticed the bath was already running. A thick bath soap I'd used in the tub to give myself foam beards was caking the entire tub, save for one spot to safely get in. The water so hot that it was steaming up the mirror and making my body sweat. Rules 2 and 3 were taken care of, it seemed.

A little freaked out but unperturbed, I took a couple of practice breaths before inhaling deep, feeling the pressure mount, and slowly stepping into the tub, careful not to let my feet slip. Even at that age, I knew I could easily hit my head on the faucet and cave my skull in.

Nothing was going to stop me from winning this game.

The water looked inviting, but murky. The thick paste had covered the top in a layer of foam with small patches of the black liquid poking through, the bottom obscured and creating an illusion of depth. As my feet touched the water, I felt the searing heat ripple through my skin, threatening to tear at the flesh.

But you'd be amazed at how determined a child can be when a prize is up for grabs.

I decided in my infinite wisdom that I'd brave it in one go. I exhaled and let my body up to my neck sink down, the pain enough to make me yelp and try to get out. But after a couple of moments, I took in one final deep breath and pushed on, submerging myself fully.

Eyes burned, and senses dulled in the inky, hot blackness. It felt like swimming through tar, but as the rules suggested, ignoring it was the only way forward. My stomach pushed in protest and muscles began to burn, but I focused on letting the current take me, not even questioning how a current was a thing in a bathtub… I did wonder, was it always this wide and deep?

I focused on the sinkhole and saw long, scaled hands protruded from either side, the nails sharp and cracked, soft flesh flapping in the water and coming off in small chunks. It started pushing at the edges of the sinkhole and widening it, my body steadily being pulled towards it as the lights above darkened and the burning in my chest became less of a problem. In fact, everything in my body relaxed, and all I had to do was float.

I saw into the sinkhole, and it took many years of reflection with an adult mind to figure out what I experienced as a child. Words still fail me 30 years later. They're inadequate and unable to capture the beauty below.

A sprawling obsidian city meshed into coral reefs that pulsated colours I recognised and many I had never seen before or since. The further I descended, the more blinding the eyes got, as if they were guiding me to land.

Further down, at the entrance to the city, two large statues loom either side of a grand throne. They're imposing, pilot lights swinging on their skulls, orbs for eyes and mouths in places they shouldn't be. One holding the tip of a sword with several spikes running the hilt, the other a grand hammer.

It's when I see the throne that I feel the burning in my chest return and something pulling me back and up.

It's empty, and yet it's not. Something is sitting upon it, but it isn't. A flickering image… or perhaps my eyes deemed it too much to bear full witness to. But I *felt* it in that moment. It knew I was disobeying the rules and saw fit to punish me.

It craned its horrific skull up towards me and as it smiled; the eyes blinded me, filling my body with such agony that my ribs felt as if they would snap under the pressure, eardrums burst, and skull split open. I felt as if I was dying.

My next memory was being in a hospital bed, unable to speak, and a tube down my throat. I was beyond terrified to be hooked up to machines and even more scared that I'd let down the babysitter, that the creature in the sinkhole was coming for me. I thrashed around until my mom's concerned face came into focus and she soothed me.

Tears stained my face, and I was faced with a long recovery, both physically and mentally. Therapists came and went. None of them believed "The Bath Game" was real. Every single one of them told me without fail that my babysitter was simply mentally unwell, had tried to manipulate me and drown me, that all I'd seen was my oxygen starved brain.

But I knew better. Even when she was sentenced to a mental institution and apologised for deceiving me, I knew better. I never deviated from that one pervasive thought that'd burrowed into my brain like a parasite.

I'd failed the game.

I bring this all up because I know *SOMEONE* has experienced this. They must have seen it. It's too specific for one person out of 7.5 billion to have gone through. Does nobody remember the way the tub expanded when you dove in? The widening sinkhole with the great hands? The weird, indescribable lights of the coral reefs beneath the tub? The fish-men statues holding artefacts of power? The sea emperor that resides between realities?

Everyone in Sturgeon says I'm crazy. They don't believe me, but I'll have proof for them soon.

I tried recreating the game myself over the years, but maybe my failure was simply too egregious, and the emperor simply won't allow me to re-take. I've caught glimpses in the steamed-up mirrors, though. Promises of what *could* be if I just show the resolve to go there again.

Thankfully, my son can do it for me. He's so excited, having grown up on the stories of what lays beneath the sinkhole in the bathtub. I made him wait until he was older to undertake the game;

I had to ensure if he told others, they wouldn't think him too young.

I sent him in about a half hour ago. I can only hope the fact he hasn't returned is proof he met the sea emperor, but he shouldn't be there much longer, right?

I want to go check on him, but because I lost, I don't think I'm permitted to interfere.

I even stood outside the door, ready to pull on the handle, but my legs won't stop shaking. I feel my throat close up and sweat run down my head. Perhaps it's a sign not to interfere?

Please… someone…. ANYONE… Tell me I'm not crazy. That I'm not alone.

Someone has to remember The Bath Game.

Because as my mind wanders and fear creeps in, all I can think of is the prize my babysitter promised, the prize my son has been promised.

Freedom.

# FURNITURE DOESN'T TALK

It is as it sounds. Incredulous as it may be, I promise there is an explanation within.

I've been the Sheriff of a little town called Sturgeon for nearly 23 years. In that time, I've seen many a horrific incident descend upon our town, fall out of my jurisdiction and get passed to the higher ups faster than you can say "nightmare scenario". It's frustrating and there's damn sure plenty of days where I feel that I'm just a prop with a fucking toy badge. But I'm still needed for the wet work, the ugly jobs and the things that stick with you no matter what your poison of choice may be.

There's a saying about gazing into the void and it gazes into you... but what do you do when the void follows you wherever you go?

Nobody is making me share this report. This account of the events that unfolded over at Caster Oil Creek deserves the light of day.

Even if it haunts me with every waking moment. A negative to my every positive.

For example, while 89% of missing persons are found, that includes dead or alive.

People go missing. Frequently. Put enough folks in one place and you're bound to have bad apples, rotten apples and things that wear the skin of apples to lure in precocious prey.

So, when people began vanishing in quick succession in Sturgeon, it was something we took notice of. I'd long suspected that it was one perpetrator, targeting seemingly at random. They left no evidence, no bodies were ever recovered, and it was always a situation where the overwhelming emotion we were left with was helplessness.

If I never have to look a grieving family in the eyes and tell them I've done all I can again, it'll be too goddamn soon. But we're a small sheriff's office and our resources are limited. This land is old and full of places we simply cannot search. Eventually, it either is open but privately declared closed… or the "higher ups" take interest and we're left fielding apologies left, right and centre.

Not this time, no. This time, it started with us and ended with us.

I need another drink. I can't face sharing this without a couple in me. Hell, y'all have no clue who I am and you're already wise to the fact I'm stalling. Sorry, context matters.

Fliers started appearing over town back in the winter of 2019. Simple, bespoke tables made by "master crafter Waylon Moseley", looking for an apprentice, a muse, and a varnisher to help him. Sales must be inquired further. When prompted, he'd brag about how his craft was passed down to him from his father and his father's father. Something about "old blood, sweat and tears" poured into every creation.

In those early days, I asked him if he kept any of his furniture or if he sold on most of his pieces. He bristled at the response before saying something that forever was etched into my mind:

"Only the ones that I connect with."

We were already dealing with a situation at the time, it was decided that a two-part sting operation, first would be to entice him with a purchase he couldn't refuse, the next would be to catch him in the act as soon as he got to his "workshop". Truth be told, we didn't know what exactly we'd find, but we knew something shady was going on. We suspected human trafficking.

We were wrong. We were so, so fucking wrong.

My hands are still shaking. Another drink should help, right? God, I hope so.

Deputy Willis eagerly volunteered for the job. He was young. Fast became my best friend. My last deputy went on maternity leave and wasn't planning on coming back, so Willis, being the happy helper, stepped up. 25 years old and wise beyond his years, he was the best little brother I could ask for. The age gap made him feel more like a son. I'd lost mine many years ago to a strange cult. Willis and my parents died young, and he was painfully shy, so I felt the need to protect him.

Still, when someone steps to the plate to do their duty and to impress you… well, it's hard to say no to that. I made him promise me he'd contact us on the transmitter the second he sensed danger. I promised him in return we'd never let anything happen to him.

I have lied many times. I have lied to my wife, to my friends and to myself. But lying without realising it at the time is the worst thing imaginable. It is a lie that will haunt me forever.

We set up shop at the Sturgeon Flea Market. A place we had very little jurisdiction within. It was decreed long ago that for things to run smoothly and with as little bloodshed as possible, compromises had to be made with the higher ups. Deals were cut, and we promised to look the other way so long as the trouble wasn't brought to our doorstep. We were up to our chests in filth and the people were either none the wiser or simply did as we did.

I hated it. Knowing that as I donned an unassuming outfit and grew out my beard for the occasion, setting up this small curio stand in the middle of a slew of entrepreneurs who dabbled in the occult, the vile and the unspeakable, I was no different from them.

After all, I was selling Willis. Perhaps he didn't see it that way, but I sure as hell did.

Once Waylon paid for him, Willis was his to do with as he wished.

He strolled up around noon. He was a lot more well kempt than I pictured. Maybe 2 decades of dealing with the ugliest of criminals gave me a biased impression of someone who I thought dabbled in human trafficking, but this guy looked… normal. About 5 foot 8, 155lbs, nice clothes if a little eccentric. His short red hair was gelled and parted to the side, his freckled smile giving off a disarming sensation. He stopped in his tracks and looked at what I had on offer—a mixture of antiques, curiosities—and Willis sat in a leather chair with his best poker face. He was told to look like he had been "broken" and he certainly gave off that impression.

The moment he laid his eyes on Willis, something clicked in him.

"He's magnificent…" he breathed, running his hands across his legs and thighs, as if inspecting a priceless artifact. I had to hold down bile as I forced a smile, remembering my training.

"You like him, kid?" I walked offer, slapping his shoulder with pride. "Well, this one was a hell of work to make, but I'm damn proud of how he turned out!"

I laughed, but my eyes fixated on Waylon, who bristled as I put force on Willis' shoulder. I couldn't figure out why at the time, but he brushed it off and reached for his wallet.

"How much?" I saw his lip quiver ever so slightly… what did he have planned for him? I wanted to tackle this fucker to the ground right there and then, but the trained words spilled out of me before I could stop myself.

"For Willis? Hm… he's a model, after all. How much ya got?" I put on my best salesman face and leaned in, disgusted at myself for how far I'd go to secure the arrest, telling myself it's for the victim's past, present and future: "He's a keeper, you know."

Waylon fumbled and pulled out 60 bucks, saying something about rent and stimulus checks not being in. I was taken aback. If he was a human trafficker… where was his cut? I stared, trying to formulate a response, but he pulled something out of his pocket before I could reply and held it in front of me.

"There's also this… it was my grandmas, it's a warding talisman. It's supposed to keep bad spirits away, it's priceless."

So, this was why we never found him.

The fucker was handing me the one thing that was keeping him hidden.

I realise to many of you, this is hokum, and I don't blame you. But where I come from, this sorta old practice does what it says on the tin: it keeps the wearer obscured. Not invisible or any kind of shit like that, but it hides them from prying eyes.

And either he didn't know what it truly did, or he simply didn't care when faced with a new model to take home.

Didn't matter, this was what I wanted.

There was nothing more to do. I took the talisman and inspected it, nodding as he took Willis by the hand and walked away.

Willis took one last look back at me, his eyes glowing with pride. He knew he was going to be the one to call it in and we'd be heroes for capturing one of Sturgeon's worst human traffickers.

As I smiled back, a chill ran through the air and practically froze my blood.

An omen.

*******

I realise to those of you following along there's been no pause in this account. But for me, I had to stop and drink myself to sleep. The closer we get to the moment it all came to a head, the more I want to put a bullet between my eyes and make it all go away.

But I recognise the public interest in what happened, and I have a duty to tell it, so we continue.

Willis' tracker was supposed to allow us to follow him no matter where he went, even if Waylon stripped him bare and gave him new clothes. It was under his skin, after all. We didn't expect Waylon to check that.

And yet, once their signal went towards The Kartuk Woods, it simply died.

16 hours had passed, and we were beginning to get antsy. It was decided we would look at the area surrounding the woods and see who lived in the area. It didn't take us long to find Caster Oil Creek and the small set of lodges out there. While Old Man Mathers was immediately ruled out, the same couldn't be said for his neighbour across the creek.

"Been in this area a long, long time." He told us on the drive up there "All of 'em. Settled here before my family did. Helped us build this here lodge for a time until my great great Grandpappy Obadiah asked them to leave. Never told us why, simply said it weren't right what they were doing over there… And now there's just one. Don't see him much, he's a solitary type… he's so involved in his woodworking, he doesn't even notice what's going on in this here creek."

We pressed him on the creek, but all he'd say was "Bad water." And refused to comment further, instead pausing and replying with, "Looks like a storms brewing. Better be ready."

We arrived at the old lodge within 20 minutes. A quiet night with the moon reflecting over the creek. Not a sound of nature or insects whatsoever as we made our approach.

You'd think with 3 cars and 5 trained servicemen, we'd be less intimidated.

But nothing prepares you for what we saw.

Breaking down the door, we were greeted with an almost ancient and rustic living room, dust littered everything, and the furniture looked so decrepit and worn down that it'd break if so much as anything touched it. The smell of rotting wood and mothballs was overpowering. I'm sure mould was a factor too, but there was something… iron-like in the air that I couldn't place.

A quick sweep of the home showed us the only non-dusty area, the large rug. Moving that aside led to a trapdoor that, with great effort, came open and lead down a large set of stairs.

As we descended, the smell of death began to grow in intensity. Our less experienced servicemen opting to hang back and cover the entrance, leaving me and two colleagues to continue.

Fuck, I need another drink. My hands won't stop shaking.

We approached what I can only describe as a leathery, undulating door. It shook in place and felt like the hide of a cow to touch; it was warm when I placed my hand against it and something… moved underneath my palm. I pushed without much force, and the door gave way.

The stench was unbearable, and my eyes watered as my stomach threatened to eject everything within it. I felt my knees begin to buckle but my resolve kept them upright. I was grateful all 3 of us had masks on, I don't know I'd have been able to cope otherwise. The room was stained in red; it'd been transformed into a living area with odd furniture lining each section of the sizeable room. A large, hairy wardrobe in the corner next to a bed that seemed to sway in place. A small chest of drawers with bizarre shelves holding a spiked lamp on top of it.

A TV sat in the centre of the room, some strange mesh coating its entire frame and a screen blaring out static that partially illuminated the room, the yellow couch with purple spots seeming to dance in the light.

To the right, however, sat cages. Some rusted over and others covered in filth and blood, but they were unmistakable.

"Got you."

There, right in the centre, clad in a stained apron and humming to himself, was Waylon, busying himself over a table with a slew of tools cast to the side.

"Waylon Moseley, you're under arrest for human trafficking." I called, trying to push authority into my voice as best I could, trying not to gag.

He put a thick tarp over the table and turned, as if in a daze, arms spread out and smiling.

"Have you come to check out my furniture, Officer?"

He laid his eyes on me, and one of my colleagues moved in to arrest him. His smile faded.

"Were you expecting someone else? A client for your illicit practices, perhaps?" I scoffed, the stains on his apron and hands telling an ugly tale.

"What is the meaning of this? What's going on? I'll have your badges, all of you!" He cried, genuinely upset that we'd barged in, as if what he was doing was perfectly normal. I took a couple of steps closer, his current project still obscured from view.

"Waylon Moseley, you're going away for a long, long time. We met a little while ago. I'm Sheriff Erickson. We did a little trade, and you gave up something you shouldn't have." I held out the talisman and saw his eyes glimmer. "This town might have some odd practices, but criminals are always the same when it comes to getting what they want, predictable…" I leaned down and grabbed his jaw with my hand, wanting him to feel the power I had. That I could break his jaw, rip out his tongue or snap his neck if I so wished. "Now, where is my deputy? Where is Willis?"

He wrestled against the officers but was no match and simply grunted before looking back at me, confused and angry.

"What deputy? You sold me a pristine table."

I felt my grip on his mouth tighten and I let go, slapping him as hard as I could.

"Don't play with me, son. You inspected him, you paid for him and took him away by hand. I watched you do it. Now I ain't gonna ask you nicely again. Where is he?"

I will never forget the sequence of events that followed. Even if I would give anything to do so.

His pupils dilated, and the eyes moved to the table hidden under the tarp. As I followed them, I felt the world fall away as a single question came into my mind. One I knew the answer to already,

*"Why were all the cages empty?"*

I repeated that question over and over as I slowly walked to the tarp. Another officer finding the light switch at the same time and illuminating the whole room. Screams and guttural retches filled the space as we saw what was in this room of nightmares. What was under the tarp?

Something did indeed sit here, but it wasn't pristine. It wasn't a table.

It was Willis.

His skin was stretched to the point that a single tap or scratch and I knew it'd split open. Translucent and thick veins visible like a macabre pattern you'd find on a mahogany table, his limbs acting as horrible legs, the bones broken and re-set to fit, his feet and hands turned into malformed stumps. The sockets were his eyes lay now nothing more than cup holders, his mouth agape and air escaping it. I don't know how Waylon did it; I don't want to know how he did it, but I swear to god I felt life within Willis. Something in him was still conscious.

A soft wheeze escaped him, faint but defiant,

*"Mercy.... Mercy..."*

My baby brother. I couldn't imagine his suffering. I just sobbed and screamed.

As we took in the surrounding room, it was apparent the rest of the furniture wasn't swaying, twitching or undulating. It was all still alive. It was people. Poor, unfortunate people Waylon had entrapped and re-designed using his "master craftsman" technique, making them into his living, be-spoke furniture of horrors.

And that was the part that terrified me the most.

*******

We hauled him away. The entire time he protested his innocence, that he was simply acquiring old furniture and restoring it. He also insisted someone had set fire to the building, and he was outside when we apprehended him. I don't know if he was mentally trying to distance himself from what he'd done, removing his past deeds somehow, but I don't fucking care.

I had to tell Willis' wife what happened to him. I lied and said Waylon simply killed him and dumped his body when he found out he wasn't useful. I couldn't bear them knowing he was a part of Waylon's furniture, not even after the news got out.

We'd find out as time went on who some of the victims were. An ex-girlfriend here, an old dorm-room buddy there, a couple of travellers he'd taken in and several missing persons from the entertainment district. All in all, we found nearly a dozen missing persons in his home. A lot of families would get both closure and add new nightmares to their suffering at the same time.

We interrogated Waylon for 3 straight days, but not once did he break his mentality that what he'd done was wrong. He genuinely did not see any of his victims as people, but as furniture for him to save.

After that final interrogation, I wanted to hand in my badge after Waylon's sentencing, leave Sturgeon and settle down somewhere quiet. I couldn't face both his last words and the recollection of our first call with him, what it meant for the wider consequences. But it was that feeling that made me stay, to catch the next embodiment of evil before he or she strikes.

You see, Waylon was very forthright with his business, explaining that he, in fact, did sell on most of his pieces to wealthy clients. Never asked details, just that they took care of his pieces and paid him appropriately so he could "live his dream." He told us in that call he only kept the "ones he connected with." Like a true fucking freak.

But it was that final response he gave before he was taken away that keeps me drinking, keeps my hands shaking and a lifelong hatred of the evil this world houses. I will never forget the way his eyes lit up, the curling of his lips, or the way his tongue caressed his teeth when he replied.

We'd asked him if he was concerned about the fact that not only had one of his victims had gotten away before being twisted beyond recognition, ready to testify against him in an already ironclad case, but that Willis was able to speak in short, pain wracked sentences and give his own account. That, if and when found guilty, he'd be given one of the worst punishments imaginable.

I can still hear his response in my ears every time I lay my head down, joining Willis' pain-riddled wheezes as a chorus of hatred and pain.

It will haunt me for the rest of my fucking life:

"No, because furniture doesn't talk."

# HONK IF YOU'RE HUNGRY

*"HONK IF YOU'RE HUNGRY!"*

A portly, haggard clown stood opposite, clutching a pathetic sign from rotting cardboard with crude marker scribbled across the front. His putty-stained gloves and sour facial expression gave the whole thing an even weirder vibe. His frayed white outfit was smeared with red, black and grey putty, some of it practically dripping off of him as he moved his body at awkward angles to accommodate the feats of the cardboard.

"What the fuck…" Jesse and I exchanged a look of bewilderment at the absolute state of the man some twenty feet away from us in the rapidly dwindling parking lot. It was late, there'd been a phenomenal concert across the street where my ever-daring friend Jesse got a little too rowdy and had his face kicked in. We were absolutely engrossed in his hilarious wincing before the sound filled our ears, the smell assaulted our nostrils and our eyes felt like they needed bleaching after reaching the source.

"Bro, I don't think you mean hungry…" Jesse began, still clutching his nose and sounding almost comically congested. "I think you meant honk if you're horn—OW!" I punched him hard in the ribs and refused to break eye contact with the Meat Clown as he gingerly twirled the sign around, the cardboard threatening to shatter like his pathetic frame at any moment.

He took a step forward, the tarmac looking like it'd swallow his sad existence whole at any moment. His eyes transfixed on me and Jesse as a soft gurgle began parting his lips and working its way through the air, into our ears.

"H… k" it carried on the wind, but it wasn't strong enough to make out. I thought maybe he was coughing as Jesse continued to bitch and moan.

"What the hell, Rich?!" He rubbed his arm dramatically, barely paying attention to the meat clown shuffling towards him. But I was. Something about him just felt… off.

He started to sway from side to side and closing that gap slowly but surely. My hair stood on end. Jesse, on the other hand, fuelled by adrenaline, walked confidently towards him, and held out a hand to his ear.

*"Tell me a joke, brother Penny!"* He bellowed, fully expecting laughter to break out at any moment.

But it didn't.

"H…o…k" The sound became clearer, each consonant gurgled out in a guttural drone, his eyes wide and piercing amid a sea of white makeup and thick black eyeliner, a red sigil painted on both sides of his cheeks and joining down at the chin. He edged closer, gripping the sign tightly, nails digging into the cardboard. One started to peel away as it was forced further in, black rotting flesh poking out from underneath.

"You'll have to speak up my man. So far, your outfit is way funnier than your routine!" Jesse bellowed, slapping his thigh dramatically and laughing.

But when the clown kept walking closer, his laughter petered away very quickly. Before I'd even had a chance to close the gap and pull Jesse away, this macabre mascot was face to face with him… literally. I immediately walked towards them sensing danger, but with every step came new clarity on his features and I'm ashamed to say I slowed down when I heard him properly.

"Honk" was all he emitted. But it was guttural, low, elongated. Like a rumble in his diaphragm that his throat was barely able to push out beyond a croak, the last gasp of a dying soul rushing to leave a decaying corpse. His eyes were the sole thing on him that looked alert. The white paint wasn't white paint, it was sallow malnourished skin stretched to the absolute brink over gaunt cheeks and frail limbs. His outfit's putty was covered in flies and maggots. The stench was enough to make me gag. Jesse stood frozen in horror as the clown pressed his face directly onto his, unblinking as he continued his bizarre and unnerving cry.

As I pulled Jesse back by the scruff of his neck, a sickening squelch sound followed by a snap cut the air and stopped the bizarre honk.

It was a portion of his nose. The gangrenous flesh was still attached to Jesse as he screamed and pulled at it, desperate to get it off of his face, though the Clown seemed completely nonplussed by the issue. He simply bowed, wiped his hand, and held the sign up, walking away from us and towards a small food shack at the far-end of the parking lot, where the woods began. It had a few benches with some people sitting around it and black smoke was billowing out of its chimney top, but the inside was a mixture of too far and too dark to make out.

*"Dude, that is the grossest prank ever, this isn't YouTube!"* Jesse shouted after him, but clearly too frightened to pursue. He finally ripped the flesh off of his nose and stomped on it, calling it "shitty putty" as he did.

But as we got a little bit further away, the same sound rang out again. A guttural, almost muffled and elongated honk. The noise filled the empty parking lot, and I looked around for its source, unlocking the truck as I did so.

"Jesse, the fuck you think he is?" I asked, craning my neck as if somehow the weird fucker had grown wings and turned into the ultimate nightmare fuel for any sane person, a flying clown.

When I turned to look back, expecting Jesse to be halfway into the car and grabbing the aux chord so he could blast my ears with Code Orange, I saw him kneeling on the floor and clutching at his stomach.

"I'm… I'm so hungry…" He winced, pulling at his stomach and his head shaking profusely. I thought he was having some kind of food poisoning moment and didn't know if I should move him or give him some room for the impending explosion. But before I could even move, I heard that sound again, clearer, and more pronounced.

Jesse was making it.

I looked at him and while still clutching his stomach, his mouth hung open and the noise rang out, filling my ears and giving me goosebumps. Not knowing what else to do, I helped him to his feet and started towards the truck.

"C'mon, I've got food at mine, if that's what you need. But I really think you should go to the hospital…"

"NO!" He pushed me away with surprising strength. It took me aback. I stared at him in shock as his face grew wild, instinctu-al… maddened. "I *need* to eat. That's too far… But there's that place… right there…" He pointed a shaky finger to the shack that the mascot had wandered off to. "That will do, it's not far. Come on." He winced again before setting off.

"You want to follow what could be the end result of Pennywise fucking a Zombie? Dude… he *just* freaked you out. He freaked *me* out. Can't we just get food at home?" If I'm honest, I was pleading more for me than him. Clowns bothered me at the best of times. But this one being devoid of joy entirely set me off all the more. Jesse wasn't having any of it, though. He sauntered off and spoke less and less as we got closer.

The shack had a dingy sign written above it, but it must have been in another language or made up of the same symbols on the clown's cheeks, because I couldn't make heads or tails of it. It was pretty sizable and there was no car attached, instead it was just placed directly onto the concrete with huge metal clamps on the corners jutting out. The cook must have been absent as the inside was pitch black, save for some swift movements from something inside. The benches had a couple of homeless people sleeping on them, but given the part of the city we live in and the late hour, I sadly wasn't surprised.

That rotting stench hit me again as we got closer and I had to hold back vomit, covering my mouth and my nose with my sleeve.

"Oh my god… Jesse, can't you smell that?!" I called, but he was practically rushing to the table and ringing the bell. "C'mon man, they're obviously closed, we should—"

A fucking plate with a stack of discoloured meat appeared before my fucking eyes. If there were a pair of hands doing the work, I didn't see them. Jesse didn't even wait to pay, just left his wallet on the side, and took the food to the nearest bench, gorging himself on the rancid meat and moaning.

I tried to get closer, but the smell was overbearing, the assaulting stench of sweetness and putrid meat.

"Wait in the truck, I'll be ready as soon as…. as soon as I'm… oh my god *yes*" Jesse was drooling between bites, thick globs of saliva as he scarfed the food down, almost choking before continuing. I was so light-headed at the time, that I didn't think it'd be so bad if I went for a quick drive to clear my head. I nodded and rushed away from the smell as fast as I could, desperate for clear air.

Turning on the AC and putting some piano music on, I tilted back the driver's seat and rested my eyes for a few minutes. I could feel my stomach protesting, every growl reminding me that while there was food nearby, I sure as hell wouldn't have it. I grabbed my stomach in protest, but it simply growled more, every twitch like a finger prodding against the flesh. The sound shifted and changed, the hairs on the back of my neck standing on end.

"Hooooonk."

I came to before I'd opened my eyes and I'm so thankful I didn't immediately do so. I could hear the groans, the dripping of the meat. The gaudy, shambolic outfit.

He was in the car. The meat clown was in the fucking car. His decaying body leering at me, making that fucking noise.

"Hooooooonk."

It sounded like a death rattle, the sort of thing you'd hear someone say when it's their final breath before passing on. I heard a sound I couldn't place, like the sound of a wet bag being dragged along the concrete. I looked down and spied a chunk of grey sludge being pulled from his pockets, directed towards my face. I could see it undulating. I wasn't about to let him put that shit on me, so I instinctively leaned my head forward and smashed it into his.

I immediately regretted my choice.

I missed, a punch to the tide of the temple left my ears ringing and my eyes blurred. Adrenaline was the only thing fuelling me at this stage.

But as I turned to scream at him to get out, I saw his face.

Wide eyed and with a switchblade to his eyelids, he was rapidly slicing through them with remarkable precision and skill. All the while, making that dreadful sound, but it was changing.

"Hooooonkrrryyyy," he hissed as he split one eyelid free, the eye rolling in its socket, he started on the lower one as I stood frozen in fear and horror. In less than 30 seconds, both eyelids were gone, and he cut the soft stalk, holding the eye in one slice before cupping it in his hands, still making that sound.

He put the hand out toward me as I rapidly scooted away. I could see the eyelids and the eyes were rotted, fetid and decayed. He persisted, pushing it towards my mouth until I had no room to move. My hand reached for the handle and all my weight fell out and back onto the concrete. My skull hitting the concrete with a thud.

The next thing I knew, he was holding me down as he forced his hand down on my mouth as it filled with soft meat. He pushed hard on my jaw against my will and as it burst in my mouth, I felt my vision fade and the world around me shake, his expression never changing as that sound carried me into unconsciousness.

"Hooooooonkrrrryyyyy."

The first thing I felt when I awoke was pure disgust. I wretched and tried to vomit, but it wouldn't come up, not even when I put my fingers down my throat, as if there was nothing in my body to regurgitate.

Now he was in the driver's seat, the clock showing it'd been 3 hours since I'd left Jesse. I couldn't taste anything in my mouth and there seemed to be no damage to the car, so I chalked it up to a horrific nightmare.

Concern overtook confusion rapidly, and I got out of the truck to find Jesse, it was still early hours and the place looked even darker than before, but in the short time it took to reach the food truck, I could see FAR more people aimlessly wandering around, some on the benches and others congregating. Was there a late-night craving or something? Maybe the bars had just let out, and they wanted that drunken fast-food experience.

The rotting stench from earlier was totally gone, too. I could smell the succulent aroma of sizzling bacon, tender crispy chicken, a medium-rare steak, and flavours that took me straight back to being a kid again. My dad making a BBQ on a summer's eve and playing Nintendo while I happily ate and kicked my feet. God, I wanted that feeling SO badly, I couldn't help but feel hungry in that moment. Captured by the memory, I was so lost in the moment that I almost missed Jesse.

When I snapped out of it, I saw him. All of him.

He was still eating, his jaw locked and ripping at the hinge, muscles still pumping and the tongue lazily drooping over the side as gnarled hands shoved more cold meat into his gullet, the throat akin to that of a duck and just absorbing it into his frame, not even properly chewing. But the eyes were vacant and milky, the nostrils weren't moving, and his stomach was bloated.

Whatever was pushing him to continue eating, it'd taken his soul with it. This was no longer Jesse, this was something else. Something horrifying.

I looked around, wondering why nobody had stopped him or called for help. But when one of the women passed me, I noticed the similarities between her and the Meat Clown: sallow skin, sunken eyes, gaunt features… all signs of pure malnutrition and a zombified state. What the fuck was I in the middle of? The smell was overbearing in much the opposite way from earlier, threaten-ing to take me away into another beautiful memory and making my stomach squeeze and groan in protest, but I fought to keep focused, my shock the only thing stopping me from crying at the sight of my dead friend.

Something cut the air, though. It ripped through it and every person surrounding me perked their ears up and snapped their eyes to where Jesse sat. It sounded like someone stamping on a packet of sauce; it was squishy and followed by a distinct pop and a wet thud.

Jesse's stomach had ripped open, his entrails scattering on the floor and in his lap. Immediately the people around rushed to him, knocking me aside as they fought each other to grab at the plates scrape or, in a truly barbaric fashion, pulling at his entrails and squeezing out pieces of digested meat to savour.

I stumbled back until I bumped the counter of the truck, hitting the bell with a horrid "hooooonk". Snapping around, I saw the sign in clear English: *"Pav' Loves Meat."*

Just like before, a pair of unseen hands rushed to attention as the smoke billowed and a smell so overpowering filled my lungs and made me cry, the violence 10 feet away a distant memory. Even the Meat Clown's distant, horrifying smile wasn't enough to sour my mood or my craving for that memory food again. Nothing was.

*******

There was a small package in my hands. I didn't realise I was even holding it, not until I was back in my car. Sunlight will be creeping over the horizon soon and I've no doubt people will ask where Jesse is, but I doubt they'll ever find him.

The package is a small to-go box, wrapped in foil and still hot to the touch, the smell making me smile when it wafts my way, the emotion like looking at a puppy you're taking home after losing your former best friend.

The issue I'm faced with now is that in addition to the horrific hunger I can feel building in my stomach, I can look around and see people going about their early morning routine.

Each one of them with that same sign the Meat Clown is holding, all of them directed at me.

"HONK IF YOU'RE HUNGRY"

I can't see the food truck, the people, Jesse, or anything else but the signs and the visions of better days with better food.

I can only hear the honking.
And I am so…so… hungry.

# THE SCHOLAR OF SKIN

Everyone stumbles into *that part of YouTube* once in a while. You're sleep deprived, maybe anxious or just bored and in what seems like an instant you're transported from watching an innocuous video from your favourite YouTuber about life or gaming and you're on the 8th or 9th video of thick calluses being peeled, pimples being popped, and hooves being trimmed.

DrPimplePopper, TheToeBro, NateTheHoofGuy and The-HoofGP, among countless others, showcase their talents for all to see. It's the 2022 equivalent of channel hopping and finding yourself on the late-night gruesome medical stories or police chases gone wrong shows.

Maybe nostalgia keeps me here just as much as morbid curiosity?

Some don't like to admit they enjoy the almost cleansing sensation of watching someone's feet addled with sores and yellow, flaking skin, being steadily worked on, and cleaned until only fresh skin remains. Same goes for growths, pimples, extractions, and the aforementioned hoof trimming.

I won't condescend you by explaining fully what hoof trimming is. Cow's feet get overgrown and professionals step in to ensure they get trimmed in a manner no different to us clipping our nails. Something about them removing the dirty skin to reveal the soft white flesh underneath is just addictive in its nature.

In any case, it's when watching one of these videos underneath a thick blanket in the dead of winter where my situation begins. I usually watch these with a bunch of friends on discord. We all have that weird interest in strange videos, and this is just a small section of it. Any of you in a group-chat know that even the most mundane of content is enhanced with a bunch of your friends reacting to it in real time with you. Plus, with the current circumstances, it's a superb way to stay connected.

Nevertheless, when I hopped on after a night shift expecting them all to be there, everyone was offline save for Mika, who was sat muted in the group-call. I tried to get his attention, but he must've fallen asleep.

I put the broadcast function on and began watching, hoping that maybe the others would wake up eventually and join in. I checked "general" and saw our other friend, Devon, had posted the new playlist link. Clicking it, I got comfy and prepared for the ensuing weirdness.

It was from a privately listed set that had a handful of new views.

"WHAT'S HIDING IN THIS COWS HOOF?" Was the title, a standard photo of the damaged hoof with a big yellow arrow pointing to it, posted by a new account: The Scholar of Skin.

Strange and given this is a hoof video, not entirely accurate, but there's definitely been weirder ones out there and I assumed he started with callous videos before moving onto hoof trimming for max viewership. The video loaded up with no title sequence, a standard GoPro camera already in place on the tripod as it stared down at the hoof held up in the crush, a mechanism that keeps the cow safe and still, hoisting up each leg using a series of levers.

"Welcome back fellow scholars of skin, it is I: Your esteemed professor, asking you to kneel at the pulpit as today we're at Sturgeon Dairy Farm and we have a lesson on the importance of regular hoof trimming, particularly with these new kinds of bovine." He cleans off the muck from the hoof and when finished extends a gloved hand, a long thick finger jutting out and pointing at the soft spot which he pokes and prods as the cow mooed. "Underneath here is a legion that has burst and caused the hoof capsule to separate from the corium. In layman's terms, all of these hoof horns are no longer attached to the delicate flesh it's protecting. This can happen when these cows are going through their lives and for multiple reasons, but we know why on this occasion."

He pulls out a sharp knife and begins slicing away at the old, disconnected hoof, the feeling of cleansing washing over me as dirty and old horn is discarded and making way for the fresh skin to breathe. I suppose one could get the same enjoyment from watching potatoes being peeled, but this was far more satisfying.

He cut away in silence for a couple of minutes and my eyes looked around the shot, to the small bits of the room I could make out. Something felt… off about it, but I couldn't put my finger on what before he began speaking again:

"…And here is the live flesh underneath, now we don't wanna cut that, but in order for this cow to truly heal and become what they're meant to be to the farmer, we have to make some difficult decisions." He lifts the last bit of hoof hiding the corium and slices it away, a strange yellow substance underneath where the brown and pink flesh should reside. The cow made a guttural sound, as if in pain. Though most of these videos will always assure you the cow, while scared, isn't in any major pain… this one felt sincere.

I sat up and mouthed "what the fuck" as he seemed to respond in kind.

"You see it too, don't you? This cow hasn't quite finished its maturity yet. The inside of the hoof capsule isn't fully doing its job. It's being rejected by this delicate tissue underneath. Maybe the cow in question simply doesn't have what it takes to mature… A pity, he was a feisty one and would've made for good stock." He sounded more amused than sad, his obscured face breathing heavily with the cold air around him fogging up the lens for a moment. As he wiped it, the camera tilted, and I clocked onto why it seemed off.

My skin began to itch from head to toe, my scalp burned, and my legs shook as two horrible realisations overcame me.

The first was that he wasn't on a farm. There were no swathes of livestock, no stable, no other signs of life. It was a sterile black room, like some rented out warehouse with floodlights. The only thing within view was the crush itself and the cow attached.

The second was the mooing. It took a couple of times to realise, but it wasn't that of a cow. It was too high pitched, too wailing in its tone and almost had a vibrato to it.

Like the way someone's pleas for mercy would be when in great pain.

"Shall we take a look at the handsome lad before we give him back to the farmer for processing?" The Scholar cooed, a soft almost innocent chuckle escaping his lungs as he picked up the camera and walked around the crush, ensuring the viewer got every bit of the body in shot from back to front.

It was like watching a live leak video of a car accident or some other kind of tragedy. Every part of you wants to click off, to shut the laptop or close the tab and scrub your skin until it bleeds, to remind yourself there *can* be good in the world and erase the images from your mind.

But you can't. Fear grips you to the seat like it did to me. A cold sweat eases the feeling of itching on your scalp, but your stomach is eating itself out of anxiety as your fingers pick at each other for sustenance.

The back legs were that of a cow, that much was clear. But the further along the camera went, the clearer it was that this was not a cow. The legs joined at a pair of flesh coloured, humanoid hips, the torso sporting a distended stomach with withered and rotting udders where the skin split to accommodate, some patchy fur growing in. As the camera panned to the front, I saw the terrified, milky eyes of my friend Neil, drool constantly escaping his lips like a broken faucet and his human ears hacked off, dipped in black and sewn further up his head.

I could not tell if he was still possessing his faculties, but he knew full well who the man was in front of him, and his eyes rolled into the back of his skull as The Scholar approached.

"You were a disappointment, number 992. You can't even moo properly, can you?" He leaned in and grabbed the slobbered, slack jaw of my friend, slapping his face and making him look directly at the camera. "Moo for me. Moo for the audience. Moo for a million subs. Moo for your life."

Neil did as he was told. Tears streaming down his face as the most god-awful death rattle of a moo left his lungs, his back legs kicking and something unseen splashing to the ground behind him as The Scholar laughed.

"Good, good. I hope the farmer is happy enough to give you more time, son. Otherwise... well, he knows I like it medium rare." He laughs again as he pulls a few levers and the crush begins moving, pulling all the limbs of Neil into horrifying positions as he walks away, a few moments of darkness before standing by a light switch. "Hopefully he'll make a better meal than he did as a guest here. Can't wait to see you on the next video!"

He hits a light switch that blinds the screen for just a moment before it cuts to the outro, leaving me in a panicked state. I called the authorities and, while on hold, I checked back into the discord.

All of my friends were still offline save for Mika, who was saying something so softly I couldn't hear it, but making enough noise that the green light around his avatar lit up.

"Mika… Mika, what the fuck was that? Is that… is that fucking Neil?? Are you playing some weird prank on me? Dude, I'm on hold to the police right now, so you better fucking explain yourself!"

A faint knocking could be heard in the background, and it was enough to make me check my own door. Still locked, nobody there. I kept my headset on as I walked back and again pressed Mika to talk.

"He… He knows, Josh." He whimpered, his voice barely above a panicked whisper. "He uploads regularly, and he knows we've been watching. We got the link while you were on night shift this week. Someone sent it to Neil, and we binged them, leaving comments about how much we loved the detail. He always responded in character, told us we'd be welcome to visit anytime, and he'd be watching. We thought it was some weird horror ARG and we just… fuck, we didn't catch on to begin with. He's so clever, Josh."

Again, a knocking at the door, more pronounced and the sound of Mika moving quickly to somewhere else, the mic whipping around as he settled and began crying.

"You can't be serious, dude. This is some SFX shit, right?"

"Neil came into the call, said this was a professor of skin and he noticed us, studied us and said we would be great candidates. Neil went up and said he got paid well for helping out, said there was nothing like getting up close and personal with it. Stew and Dom went next, then Ray… now it's just us. He told me… if I shared it, he'd leave one of us. I don't know what happens to us, Josh, but I don't wanna find out." He started sobbing, dry heaving as the door began to slam hard with someone's full weight against it. "He can track you just by watching it, it's not YouTube. None of us fucking paid attention. Why isn't he coming for you? Oh, fuck… oh fu—"

Mika left the call as I sat there, breathing shallow and an unwavering sense of doom in my head. That was 2 days ago. After calming down a bit, I sent the link to the authorities, and they said they'd investigate it, that it's not uncommon for phishing scams and other kinds of malicious practices to take place by disguising themselves with familiar web links. It's in their hands now.

As for me, I stocked up on groceries and kept my door locked since, making sure to keep a close eye on everything around me. I took the time to collect my thoughts and share them here, hoping someone with a bit more of a detective mind can figure out if anyone else has experienced this.

But, as you can imagine, there are a couple of problems.

The first is one that's hard to admit: I can't stop watching the videos. I know it's macabre, it's fucked up, and it puts me at risk, but something inside me just cannot stop.

I hate it. It fills me with an ungodly dread just sitting there with the dim hue of my phone screen, computer monitor or tv as The Scholar of Skin mutilates more "cows' hooves". Sometimes I recognise them and many, many times… I don't.

But if I try to stop, the dread only gets worse. The fear crawls up the inside of my stomach and nests in the back of my skull, making every single movement by myself or inadvertently around me akin to that of a fucking bomb going off.

Like I *know* I'll be next if I stop. That he'll turn up and take me.

The only thing that keeps that overwhelming fear at bay is another video.

I keep saying "just one more" and my hand moves of its own volition, clicking the play tab each time I instinctively try to stop. If I get up to use the bathroom, it's playing on my phone. If I try to sleep with the laptop closed and phone off, it's playing on the TV.

I can't stop. Even while gathering my thoughts for all of you here, it was in the background the entire time, bringing me equal parts fear, stress and a tenuous tranquillity broken by any kind of simple action not involving watching more.

But then there's the other problem, one that I'm putting off dealing with by editing my thoughts before sharing it with you all in the hopes someone, anyone, has advice for me or can bring me comfort:

There's a knocking at my door.

Why they came, what they want.

Fresh content.

And I can't stop watching.

# CLOUDCATCHER COMETH

I'm a professional cloud watcher. Only one left that I know of, in fact. I'm sure there are others watching their own skies for information and signs, but at least for my little corner of the Earth… it's just me.

Ol' Sam the cloud watcher, as they call me. Or just the oddball staring up, mouth agape at the sky. That too.

But I'm coming here in the hopes that someone else can shed some light on recent occurrences. Perhaps another cloud watching enthusiast or licensed professional?

As the title suggests, one of them has followed me home.

And I'm unsure as to how to get rid of it.

I realise how strange it sounds, to be a *professional* cloud watcher. After all, isn't it just staring up at the sky? How hard can that be? Sounds relaxing, actually!

Well, there's a bit more to it and it boils down to the same thing any profession requires: aptitude.

While almost everyone loves watching clouds, very few actually see what the clouds mean, what they are concealing and what that spells for the future of the area those particular clouds are formed over.

It's not something you learn, not at first anyway. You have to see the patterns naturally before it can be cultivated. You see it all the time in films, a couple or some friends are laying down cloud watching. They see shapes in the clouds like food, animals or sometimes what they *want* to see. It's the latter that shows something special.

I was always fascinated by the clouds. My father would scold me for constantly daydreaming and losing myself in the skies and subsequently failing my tests at school.

But one day, I pointed something out to him in the sky, looming behind a particularly large, bright cloud obscuring the sun.

"That one there, there's a catcher behind it. You can see its hands peering out from the corner. I think we're going to get a storm soon."

My dad looked at me, bewildered, and told me that there was no such thing inside the clouds, that he could only see the usual bland shapes and designs.

He sent me to bed without dinner, even as I protested that we had to take shelter, shouting to the rest of our family and neighbours until he placated me with promises of a father-son trip if I stopped this cloud nonsense.

I awoke that night to the sounds of billowing winds uprooting trees, thunderclaps that burst the eardrums and bursts of horrific ball lightning ripping through the streets below. By the time my family realised what was going on, it was too late.

Within 17 minutes, my little town, formerly known as Great Salmon, had been decimated. I was found in my bed, amid a ton of wreckage, bruised but alive and repeating "cloud catcher" over and over.

I was taken in, educated and my gift for cloud watching grew. I was sought out by other small towns for predicting the weather, helping to prepare for threats and what unusual clouds would entail. It's been a good way to live for some time. I get to help others and I get to relax, watching the clouds in the process.

Problem is, the latest town I'm helping to cloud watch for has a more unique weather situation.

Most of you will have seen all manner of cloud formations without really considering it for more than a few seconds, heavy dark clouds rolling in as a storm approaches, a blanket of grey and white obscuring the sun for a chilly day, speedy white battalions giving way to small slithers of radiant blue on a summer's afternoon and so forth.

But what do you do when the clouds you watch don't conform to any of that? What do you do when the clouds bring with them a life of their own?

The mayor of this town reached out and implored me to come and visit, said that once every summer solstice they were besotted by an unknown weather calamity that came in 3 stages over 3 weeks, ending with untold destruction and death to the town. They could never see anything more than "just the clouds" but knew something was lurking up there. They said if I could find out what it was before the final stage, I could save a lot of lives.

How could I refuse to help? And I won't lie, the prospect of something... new lurking in the clouds was most certainly enticing.

My first day on the job here involved my usual ritual: park up on the highest hill overlooking the town with an opportune vantage point, drink some Fiji water, and play some vaporwave while I sat on the hood of my car and took notes.

To help put into context what I saw and for why I've come to you all today, here's some of the more relevant logs. For the sake of time, I'll only show a handful:

### Day 1: Blue sky, white clouds.

**1hr:** Their density is thick, they march in a structured formation to the west, their generals up front with tendril-like white edges to their almost marshmallow base. They rush past me but carry no breeze. Small patches of the sun's light eke out from between the bars the clouds keep it behind, permitting next to no contact with the outside world. If I didn't know any better, I'd say the clouds were patrolling the skies, keeping something at bay.

**3hr:** There's a single conglomerate of blackened clouds rolling in, a gang from another turf, perhaps. They take no prisoners as they bullhorn their way through the nearby docks and capsize a couple of fishing boats in the process, staining the grounds with black, viscous tar. I hear a car nearby swerve and crash. I hope they're okay. I see the thin gap of blue sky rapidly being dispersed, the white clouds converging around it as if to defend it. Something in the general clouds begins to stir and I sense a bitter wind on the horizon.

**4hr:** It is almost sunset, but there is no lavender sky or palette of beautiful colours to marvel at. Instead, I watch the black clouds push in until they are nearly overhead, their anger felt by every citizen in the town below. So many are covered in the black tar that brought me here, though I didn't believe it when they told me. It cakes the great spires and oozes through the windows. The people here call it "the slow rot" and won't tell me what it does to anyone who comes into physical contact with it. There is a clear line between the bright and grey clouds and that of the dark ones. Something in the lead black cloud moves and a brilliant spark of red ripples through its body, sparking all the way down the ranks before depositing its contents, a sea of red descends on the town and mixes with the black tar, causing it to bubble and fizz like acid. When it is finished, the clouds depart as quickly as they came. I can still hear people screaming as I drive back to my lodge.

## Day 5: Yellow Sky, Yellow Clouds.

**1hr:** I got here at sunrise, the last few days bringing with them a strange set of stairs that start by the steps of the hill and ascend far beyond the perceivable clouds. There's a smell of barbecues and freshly cut grass on the wind. An attempt at bringing forth nostalgia from within me? Who can say, but the sky has concerned me for some time. Why is it yellow? I don't mean it's simply a sunny day, I mean the blue hue that was here from the first day has long since been erased and in its place sits an almost artificial yellow. I can no longer tell *where* the sunlight is coming from and something in that realisation is most unsettling. It feels like I've been to an exhibit housing a dangerous creature and now the cage is either empty or covered with a cloth and I am assured it is still there, even when I don't hear anything.

I won't lie. I do wish to go up those stairs, but I am not willing to just yet. I must understand what this all means first.

**3hr:** I must have looked away for no more than 15 minutes in order to check my logs and any info on strange anomalies in the sky. But when I looked back, the stairs had vanished, and the clouds had completely restructured. Great mountainous pillars littered the sky and continued for untold distances in either direction. As my eyes followed to the centre, my jaw dropped and my skin grew taught, bumps forming and every hair standing on end.

A small set of buildings and strange structures comprised a denser, more malleable cloud material hung in the sky overhead. Both feeling as if I could reach out and touch it, but also impossibly far above me. I followed from the entrance archway up to a longhouse, the doors slowly opening and releasing the light that was missing from the skies.

Within, I caught a glimpse of something. I... can't be sure what it was, but I know that in the few seconds I locked eyes with it, the colour drained from the clouds and a chill ran through me that was so biting I had to look away and grab a sweater to cover up. When I looked back, the clouds had become a pallid grey and covered the sky completely.

**7hr:** I slept up here. During my dream, I'd floated up to the clouds and stood at their grand archway. The colours were a rich purple and lavender. I felt at ease, communicating with some entities that were neither here nor there… dream logic, I suppose. They told me they appreciated my willingness to understand them, to study them and help "those down below", but that the solstice brings with it a new beginning and that cannot be stopped.

Still, they said, I must speak with "them" and see for myself.

I was led into the longhouse. It was far bigger in person, fit to hold something several hundred times my own size. The "beings" didn't venture too close to its interior, seemingly intimidated. As I walked its great halls, obelisks of clouds and shapes of creatures I'd never seen, I found myself at the foot of a throne made from ash and fog, the seat a constant churning thunder.

I could not tell you if something was sat upon it. My mind has elected to redact that information. But I do recall what it said to me in a deep, commanding voice that resonated within my bones:

"Cloudcatcher Cometh."

I went home that night and kept my curtains closed.

## Day 11: Tall clouds, green sky.

I awoke with a start, the sounds of cicadas shrieking an efficient alarm clock here. It took me a few seconds to realise that something else was shrieking along with them.

As I ventured out to my balcony, I saw the town bathed in a dark hue of green. Angelic horns blasting from the depths of the clouds above as a warning siren. But nobody was heeding it below.

To my horror, the black clouds had come in from the east. Thick plumes descended from their ranks and congregated in the streets. Amalgamated shapes of humanoid creatures clad in storm cloaks and bearing lightning bolts for teeth screeched as they latched themselves to fleeing citizens, devouring them, or enshrouding them in their fog.

I could do nothing as the black clouds above smashed against the defiant greys and whites, great thunderclaps echoing around us. The grey clouds had formed huge structures with which to create a fortress around the green patch of sky. They refused to let anything near it.

The moment of truth came as the largest pillar in the grey sky arched back and swung itself over the ranks of the others, colliding with the black cloud with such force that it split the sky in two, the green sky exposed and eradicating the beasts below. In the spire off to the distance, a woman clad in black had her arms held out wide and her head tilted back, revelling in the green glow.

I felt dizzy staring out at the green sky for too long and took myself back to bed, the soft crying of the townsfolk weighing heavily on my conscience.

I didn't have the heart to tell them what I'd seen, not yet.

Before I show you this last log, I feel it important to explain what I believe is being concealed in the skies and who or what is coming after it.

It's been a longstanding belief that there are things that lurk within the deep skies. The first humans who crawled out of the caves believed the sun itself was a god, to be revered and feared in equal measure as it brought them sunlight and safety each day before the darkness came and brought instead a slew of predators that craved human flesh.

So, it's no small leap of faith to assume what is being kept in the sky above this town. A sleeping, ancient god. I don't mean a god in the sense of what traditional beliefs hold. I don't believe this is something omniscient or omnipresent. But it is powerful, and it knows that people covet its power.

Which leads me to the black clouds. To the cloud catcher I mentioned before.

There have always been people who crave power and will get it by any means necessary.

Those who have not the means themselves will frequently utilise methods of force to grab it, using any tools they see as proficient.

Tools like me.

### Day 18: Crimson Sky. Obsidian Clouds.

It is dark when I ascend to the top of the hill, but it is only 10:45am here.

The townsfolk have taken shelter underground or in the churches. I was able to relay to the mayor what the danger was and, in turn, received their gratitude.

I did not guarantee them I could fix the issue, but they seemed satisfied to know *what* it is lurking in their skies and what is coming to try and take it.

Old towns have old traditions, that much is certain. It is not my place to question them or judge them, especially when I've seen the strangeness for myself. While it can be chalked up to strange chemicals in the air, unusual weather patterns or collective hysteria, my job is to interpret and extrapolate.

And that's what I'll do.

I'd be lying if I said I knew what the cloud catcher was, but it has been known to me for some time, just as the clouds I'm familiar with have been.

I stood atop that hill, vulnerable to the elements and the burning sensation of the crimson sky. No white or grey clouds remained to shield me. The once dark clouds had now adopted an obsidian hue, solid in their structure and single-minded in their resolve to take what they wanted.

This time, I did not relent as I watched them, waiting for the largest cloud to pass over me. It undulated and split apart, ugly hands and furtive eyes peering over its edges. I don't dare speak more of what it looked like, giving it further power isn't wise. But it saw me and remembered me.

And I made a deal with it.

If it followed me away from this town, from its people who had seen untold ruin and slaughter every summer solstice for centuries, I would give it new places to feed and thrive with its kin.

It agreed, and the remainder dispersed, the singular black cloud following me wherever I travel.

Now, I bid my farewells to the town and travel to my next job, a small town not far from this one: Sturgeon.

And so, it brings me to the present. To sitting in my car on a silent, singular road clad by thick trees and a blotted-out sun that my cloud catching companion has ensured will never shine on me again.

My dreams are now fraught with this creature peering over the skies in my sleeping realm, determined that it will one day bring me into the clouds and harness my skills for itself.

It is always hungry.

And I cannot feed it forever.

If any of you out there are seasoned cloud watchers or readers of the heavens above, I beg you to offer me your advice before I reach my next destination. Before I reach this humble little town of oddities known as Sturgeon, how do I stop this black cloud from consuming me?

# THERE IS A PERSON AT YOUR FRONT DOOR

"Seriously? Again?" I grimaced at the phone rumble, turning over in my bed to look at the sleep cycle clock as I pulled the phone closer to my face.

*3:02am, cloudy outside, no breeze.*

Fucking Christ… I've barely slept.

I live in a suburbia part of the town. We usually get drunken asshats who forget to look for common identifiers of their homes and just ring their doorbells expecting a roommate, spouse or family member to let them in. Sometimes, it's a prank spurred on by bored and/or drunk teenagers during the spring break period.

And occasionally, just now and then, it's something else.

My condo has a large set of steps going up to the property, wooden decking with various bits of furniture, including a hammock and some ornamental birds adorning it. My prized blue flamingo Barry sits just in view of the doorbell camera, a trusty guard if there ever was one. The reason I got the damn camera installed was because of Barry, funnily enough. I don't know if it was wildlife or some asshole, but someone pulled him from his perch and threw him into the bushes in my yard, scratching at his paint and going for the eyes.

I figured it may have been someone looking to case the area and trial a scene to see if I reacted, but I'm a heavy sleeper most nights, so the camera was a good decision.

Keeping one eye closed so I could go back to sleep after inspecting the camera, I flipped it open to the app. I have one of those NEST Hello cameras, they've got some crazy field of vision and work well in the daylight, even if the night-time view on mine is… a little grainy at times, some weird screen tearing happens around now when I look at the footage, no clue why.

I look at the screen, and sure enough, nothing is out of place. The furniture is still there, hammock is swinging, and Barry is staring dutifully at the door.

I'm about to close the app and curse some weird glitch for waking me, when it hits me and my sleepy eye snaps open as I turn over to look clearly.

There's no breeze out tonight.

So why is my hammock swinging?

Furthermore, Barry is positioned to look out at the yard. I do it as partly an aesthetic thing and symbolically, he's the guard of the house.

*So why is he looking at the camera?*

It unsettles me. Even if he is just an inanimate object, I feel sympathy towards him as much as I do fear in this moment. This isn't special, of course. I bonded with my Roomba when I found out it gets scared during thunderstorms, but the point remains that Barry could not move himself.

So, who did?

I close the app and take a moment to steady my nerves. I'd always been a nervous wreck at the best of times, and I didn't spend money on therapy to get past trauma for nothing. I grabbed my stuffed animal and rocked myself carefully until I could slow my breathing.

*-There is a person at your front door.-*

Fuck, no. No, no no no no.

I ball my hands into fists and smack my temples an even number of times in frustration before I hold them down and, tears in my eyes, breathe once more. I remind myself I'm in control and take another tentative look at the app, feeling my skin crawl as it loads for an incessant amount of time, letting my mind wander once more.

The camera looks out onto my driveway and the adjacent road. Directly opposite is the McPherson house, and to the right of them is a small clearing into the woods surrounding our suburb. It's vast and thick. God knows why anyone would go in there. You could get lost for days, possibly permanently, if you're like me and have a minimal sense of direction. I've spent so many nights afraid I'd wake up in there one day and struggle to get home, succumbing to the elements or… encountering something in there that saw me as an easy meal.

So, when the app loads and I see something in the clearing, a long neck extending from a short body and pulling its way towards me, I don't even need to register it to have a knee-jerk reaction of throwing my phone to the floor and clenching my teeth.

Enough is enough. I'm just being irrational, stupid, overthinking it just like everyone told me before. There wouldn't have been such a scene if I'd just—

"No, I'm not doing this." I tell myself, soft moonlight ebbing in from the bedroom window, situated on the opposite side of the condo. "I'm NOT. DOING. THIS."

I look at the app, still open, and stare hard at the shape on the screen, expecting a creature or a horrifying spectre to appear.

Nothing. The road is quiet and there's nothing in the clearing. But Barry is *still* staring at me and it's unsettling me more than I care to admit. I don't like things out of their place or positioned wrong. It just… sets my teeth on edge and I feel like pulling every follicle of hair off my body when I can't alter it. It's torture.

I put on some clothes and saunter downstairs, fiddling with the triple lock on my door and getting to the latch when I hear something that gives me pause.

An ever so slight creak on the second step leading up to my condo, an older bit of wood that I intentionally left weaker. I'd love to say it was part of my master plan to catch a thief, but I just enjoyed the sound and, as I said, I hate messing with set things.

Now, however, that sound was sending a chill down my spine and a horrible thought creeped into my head:

*"What if they moved it intentionally?"*

I stepped back and carefully slid the locks back into place, watching my movements as I found a safe place to sit down in my living-room, hoping not to make a sound.

I waited a good 15 minutes in absolute silence, ears trained to the outside before I felt safe to move upstairs, my mind thinking back to the incident that set all this off.

How over a decade ago, someone started showing up at my workplace and kept telling me I was the most special person they'd ever met, that I had "such special genes" and they needed to know everything about me. They followed me incessantly wherever I went, knew all my social media accounts, even the private ones and made fresh alts the same hour I'd find and block the last, constantly spewing weird prophetic shit about how I would be the most revered member of their club.

I remember the night they broke into my parent's house, waking up to them standing over me in that weird fucking outfit, smile plastered over their wrinkled and hairy face.

I remember wondering why they were smiling as they drew a serrated knife across my thigh and pooled the blood into a small vial before dashing for the door as I screamed the house down.

The guy was a well-known nut job from the homeless community who preached about some church of the dusk walker, that he knew the "all-seeing prophet" and the police had many run-ins with him, so they found him quick enough. He was sent to prison, and that was the end of it, for him at least.

It took years of therapy and a new job in an entirely new city to placate me, and even now I struggle. All the defences in the world can't seem to stop someone when they're obsessed.

Walking back up the stairs, punching in the information to call the authorities, my phone notifies me once more:

*"There is a person at your front door."*

With shaking hands, I open the app and have to put my hand over my mouth to muffle the screams.

It's him. He's older and malnourished. But it's absolutely him. Standing on the top of the stairs and leering at me, bent over and neck cocked to the side.

But it's his neck. His fucking neck is too long. It's stretched out and there're veins all over it as it extends and pushes his head closer. Deadened eyes and a wide smile greet the camera as it gets closer.

What do I do? What the fuck do I do?

I run upstairs and pull the blankets over my head, phone still in hand, and shakily try to dial 911, but I have no idea what they'll even do if I tell them what I've seen.

The phone rings out for what feels like forever when I hear a thumping sound against my window, the unfettered moonlight casting a shadow on my blankets that scars my mind and shocks me into silence.

His head is smacking against the windowpane. Either in an attempt to get my attention or, more likely, to get inside.

Hands pull at the hairs on my head, and I dig my face into my knees, begging for it all to stop with every ounce of willpower I can muster. I rock there back and forth for an age, just repeating the same thing over and over, almost in tandem with his bumps.

"Stop it, go away. You're not welcome."

It takes some time, but the bumping inexplicably stops, and I hear a snapping sound, followed by a low, desperate groan.

I feel tears run down my face and blood from where I'd bitten my lip as I take in the intoxication of a silent night.

*"There is a person at your front door."*

No.

This is designed to break me.

Shaking hands open the app and for the first time, I can't contain my scream.

It's an eye. A single, bloodied eye with full dilation jammed up against the camera. I can see something writhing in the darkness, twisting, and dancing. Beckoning to me even as I shriek so loud that lights begin to come on at the McPherson house.

Something in the blackness is calling to me and a part of me wants to go to it. Every logical part of me feels unmitigated fear. My legs are shaking, my heart is pounding so fast that I feel dizzy as I stand, and I can barely hear anything in my ears. Yet, I still walk to the door, to whatever is calling me, eyes transfixed on the app as the strange shape beckons me.

My hand slips off the first lock, the shape is no clearer, and yet I feel a familiarity within it, the contours in the eye almost inviting.

The second lock clicks in release and a rumble is audible in my ears. I feel comfort and warmth.

I pull the chain on the latch and start to open the door to my calling as the elder McPherson bellows at the top of his voice, "WHO THE FUCK ARE YOU? GET AWAY FROM THERE!"

And a shot rings out that snaps me into consciousness, hand still on the latch but pulling open the door as a blackened hand slips back through the gap in the door, a horrific howling as it darts off for the treeline, more shots ringing out as I swing open the door, still on instinct.

The second scream sounds familiar and a hot, acidic substance pours down my shirt as my eyes blur and I fall to the ground, Mr McPherson's wife coming to my aid.

It's mine. My scream. My vomit.

What was left on the doorbell was an in-tact eye, stalk and everything, pushed up against the camera with some tape, black blood pooling on the ground, on the hammock and on Barry.

A note had been stamped next to it, something that would force me to move once again and deny any strangeness that had occurred that night. Maybe Sturgeon isn't the best town for me after all… I don't know what it is they see in me, but that question is more than enough to have me prepping to move once again: **DO YOU SEE WHAT I SEE?**

# THE ECHO IN THE WOODS

"He IS real, Fabian, he's the one who gave me these flowers! I'll prove he's real to you!" She huffed, pushing the Oleanders in my face. They were beautiful, sure, but faded on the petals and looked… off somehow, like they'd been ripped and put back together hastily.

"I'm just saying, I haven't seen him, and he never seems around when I'm with you, which is often, Nara." I said, between huge bites of my churro. It was lunch and my mom had gone all out on the sugar ladened selection that'd make any 11-year-old's mouth water.

It was the summer of 2002 and, like any self-respecting pre-teen, I was exploring the world around me and doing so with my best friend, Nara. The day started out like any other, she'd come over around 10 while I was still sleeping, talk with my mom about her paintings and then wake me up by pulling the curtains back and screaming the theme song to various shows at the top of my lungs while I buried my head under the pillow. On this day, she chose *Ed, Edd n Eddy*, with pitch perfect sound effects, much to my chagrin.

I'd relent, of course. Then we played some Melee until one of us got mad enough to tickle the other into submission and grab a bite to eat before exploring the areas around our cul-de-sac. The difference in today's routine, though, was the introduction of Nara's imaginary friend, Captain Echo. A woodland creature that Nara insisted on her life was real.

Nara was… unusual. The sort of girl who made the best of any situation she was in, turned it into a positive or, at the very least, a creative environment. She'd dye her hair bright colours, wear clothes she made herself and draw her classmates with or without their permission. Not that anyone minded, she was such a free spirit that people couldn't help but endear themselves to her. That being said, she kept virtually everyone at arm's length, as if afraid they'd catch whatever weirdness she had within her if they got too close.

That's where I come in, I don't know if it was my lack of social cues in 2nd grade or if she saw something different in me, but one look at my teenage mutant ninja turtle toys was all it took for her to introduce herself and rant on about how the green ranger was the coolest. From there, we were inseparable.

"Come on, I'll prove to you he's real, right now." She said affirmatively, sitting up from the table and grabbing her hoodie, giving my mom a hug as she ran out. "Thanks Mrs Dimeo! I'll totally marry your son one day and make food just as good for you when you're old and wrinkly!"

I chased after her, kissing my mom on the cheek before she called back, "Stay safe, if he gets hurt, you can't marry him!" laughing as she closed the door.

We ran as fast as we could to the trail behind the old church, slowing down for a moment partly to pay tribute, partly to see who would get freaked out first. There was an urban legend. Some kids ghost lived there and haunted anyone who didn't show him proper respect. Which in this case was apparently a bow/curtsy and a vocal affirmation of "We see you! We acknowledge you! We remember you!" Before waiting for 5 seconds and carrying on. Naturally, one of us would spook the other during that 5-second interval and tear off down the path with uproarious laughter at the others' expense, this time Nara taking the charge.

Soon enough, the trail turned into little more than a small dirt line amid a sea of underbrush, mushrooms, moss, and insects. The trees in my hometown were beautiful and sprawling. The further you went in, the less light seeped in from the treetops. The sort of place that made it easy to lose track of time and placement if you weren't careful with your sense of direction.

After a while, we'd reach the familiar signposts that helped us figure out how close we were to our makeshift hideout. It was a clearing in the middle of the woods we'd stumbled over at the beginning of summer, we knew it was safe to be ourselves when Nara screamed out her favourite curse word and nobody came running. Over the weeks, we made it cosier with a hammock, mini radio, a campfire and some trinkets from home. It eventually grew to be our personal sanctuary, where we could sit and talk about anything that scared us in the outside world without judgment.

I turned the corner, and she was already at the edge of our circular haven, scratching something into the stack of rocks adorning the forest's outskirts.

"Captain Echo doesn't come if you don't do the greeting properly." She said, huffing as she finished engraving something I couldn't quite make out, laying a piece of her hair and a Reese's Pieces as she stood up, hands on her hips. "He has very specific requirements. He told me last time that I couldn't bring him out if it wasn't done properly. Said it would upset the great tree, and he'd get punished."

I stared, bewildered. Was I seriously going to go along with this? We were getting older and imaginary friends were never cool when you weren't far off hitting your teens. I watched as Nara stared confidently at a gap in the clearing, waiting for something to appear.

"Nara, come on…" I began, frustration building that I'd even thought for a second something would happen. She held up a hand, waving me off, fixed on the clearing.

"Shh! He'll be here in a minute. You just need to be patient, dingus! You two are gonna get on SO well!"

"Then why have I never seen him before? Why did he suddenly turn up to you one day and now he's such a big focus of our time together?" I stared down, kicking a rock. "It feels different, now… I don't get it."

She shrugged, the wind picking up and the howl rippling through the trees, amplifying to a tenacious level and giving their voice more power, as if warning us of something.

"He just… did. I don't know why he only turned up a while ago, and he was very specific that I didn't introduce you until I could promise him you were trustworthy. But he'll know you're a good guy… the best!" She sighed, repeating "the best…" again. My frustration was getting the better of me.

"You  and I are the only ones here, we've told each other everything, you don't need to pretend he's real for me."

She spun on her heel, face a mixture of confusion and hurt, curly brown hair whipping in her face as she blew it out of her eyes.

"Why would I pretend he's real for you, or for anyone?" She glared at me. "Fabian, all I'm asking is for you to wait a few more minutes. He will meet you, I promise!"

Before I could reply, a snapping some distance away caught my attention, and we both looked back at the clearing. A shape was emerging from the darkness, hands with thick, black nails gripping into the dirt and veins popping as they pulled the lanky frame into our view. When it was 15 feet away, it reared back on its legs and towered over us, staring intently at Nara. My head barely making it to his distended stomach, deep lacerations old and new covering the torso, mushrooms and moss firmly attached to the shoulders and so deeply entrenched I could swear I saw life germinating on its surface. The back was covered in thick brown fur and the head was the skull of a bear, charred black with white indentations and markings similar to what was on the carving Nara had left. The eye sockets had been hollowed out and two black orbs hung behind them, peering through the mask. He was both fascinating and grotesque all at once, but the thing that caused me to fall back was the realisation that Nara wasn't lying.

This was Captain Echo.

Nara ran forward and gave him a huge hug, wrapping her small arms around his torso as best she could, but failing spectacularly due to the monstrous frame of the creature. Still, it displayed gentleness and mechanically lifted a hand up to pat her head, as if unsure of how humans showed affection.

"N-Nara… what… what the…" I spluttered, my throat rapidly growing dry as my mind tried to comprehend what I was looking at, my vision blurring as rationalisation failed me miserably. Nara let him go and pulled me to my feet, punching me in the arm playfully.

"Told you he's real!" She scoffed, throwing her arms out animatedly as if presenting him on a game show.

"Captain Echo is our new forest friend! He doesn't speak much, but now we have someone to show us this place when we don't wanna deal with the outside world! Isn't it great?!"

In a way, it was. I was part of something so secret and wonderful that I couldn't help but be caught up in it. I laughed, walking over to Captain Echo and held out a hand.

"I'm Fabian. It's good to meet you, Captain!"

He stared at my hand, tilting his head to the side before grunting, "Fa… bi…" and grasping my hand with dirt-filled fingers and giving it a shake. I looked back to Nara as she gave me an encouraging thumbs up.

"Why is he called Captain? Does he have an army too?" I asked, wiping the dirt off my hand as he sat down, legs tucked in, and stared at the sky.

"I dunno, it's just the name he came with, I guess. I don't make the rules!" She laughed, looking over at him. "He just… is… you know? The kids at school will never understand, but who cares about them… I have you and the Captain, that's plenty." She smiled at me and for a moment, I felt the world fall out from underneath me. Then the Captain burped, and we both fell over laughing.

Our summer continued in that way, the ritual at the beginning of the day remained unchanged, wake up to a prank, play smash, eat lunch, make vague promises of marriage to my mom, stop by the church, pay our respects and head to the haven. But from there, we would enter a world all our own. Captain Echo, in his own strange way, would show us so much of the forests. How the Trees talked, the way insects lived and died in their own huge struggles for survival, the right kinds of berries to eat, watching strange animals I'd never heard about in school as they went about their day. It was mesmerising and yet I can only remember figments of it now some 17 years later. Memory is a funny thing.

When the summer came to a close, we said goodbye to the Captain and promised we'd be back by spring. He bowed and crawled back into the deep of the forests as our lives continued. Trends would come along while Nara and I focused on our own world of comics, video games and Nara's increasingly vivid drawings, many of which were getting her attention around town for their true to life design and otherworldly elements interlaced with ordinary scenery. A young girl's hand in hand with a huge goblin as the world crumbled around her, a small boy sitting on an endless row of stairs that lead to nowhere as a disembodied hand reached out from the corner and her most revered piece, a huge burning oaken tree with branches containing human pods, each one in a different emotional state as they reacted to the burning forest around them. At the centre stood a glowing figure, arms dug deep into the ground as thick tendrils spanned out and into the far reaches of the painting, infecting it all as it went. A black and red sun hanging overhead providing a macabre backdrop to such a painting.

It was beautiful, sure, but something about it was… off. Nara looked more tired than usual. Her energy had been slowly dipping since the summer ended and I hadn't realised how extremely until we got to the new year. It'd been 6 months since we said goodbye to the Captain and while I'd felt fine, Nara was wasting away. Her once flush cheeks were sallow, hair unkempt and her demeanour so devoid of joy. I asked her about the painting, and she exhaled as if the last of the world's oxygen was leaving her for good.

"I've dreamt about it every night for a week, I guess I just had to get it out of my system." She shrugged, bags under her eyes and absently eating her lunch. I was beginning to worry. "I think I need to go into the forest again soon, see Captain Echo. I think I've been away too long."

"That's fair. I'll come with you, maybe we can look at some of those weird monkeys again!" I smiled encouragingly, but she didn't return the grin.

"No, I'm gonna go alone. I'll let you know when we can hang next, kay?" She grabbed her things and gave me a short kiss on the cheek before heading out.

I remember sitting there for a minute, hand on my face affirming that was real while also dealing with the knowledge the person I trusted most in this world and valued above all others, even my mom, had just disconnected from me entirely. I wasn't a super mature kid, but I knew that I couldn't just leave her and let her drift away.

I grabbed my things and, knowing it was too late for her to go after school and that she'd want to go when undisturbed by time constraints, waited until the weekend. It took no time at all on a particularly sunny day to catch up and reach the clearing, where an exhausted Nara was sat on the floor, knees to her chest and staring at the same clearing as always, shaking.

"Hey, goofball…" I began, startling her, but not gaining her full attention as I tentatively stepped forward. "I know you said not to come out and I'm really sorry I didn't listen, but I just—"

"You really are an idiot, Fabian Dimeo." She said, her voice broken and shaking. "You'd follow me wherever I went, even if I told you what was happening, wouldn't you?"

I stood, my stomach in knots and a hot feeling coming over my face. I hated seeing anyone upset, most of all Nara.

"Of course, that's what best friends are for, I'd never stop following!" I said, trying to inject enthusiasm into my voice and hoping it wasn't obviously forced. She sniffed, wiping her face with her sleeve, and getting to her feet as the crunching from the dark returned once more.

"Fabian, I didn't want to say goodbye. That was why I wanted to come alone! That and…" She looked nervously over her shoulder before snapping her eyes back to mine, taking a step towards me. "You can't follow me where I'm going next."

I was confused. I swallowed and tried to ask why, but no words came out. She fumbled with her hands and continued.

"I've been coming out here more and more in secret, he kept calling to me in my sleep, in my dreams… it got to the point where I was having full conversations with him that made me realise…" her eyes welled up as she took another step to me and put a hand on my face. "That this world isn't for people like me, not really. He has a place all his own that I can stay in forever. All I have to do is let go."

I didn't understand, this wasn't Nara. This wasn't the girl who pranked me at every opportunity, the girl who drew beautiful but comical and abstract art for amusement, the girl who sang her heart out whether she was on her own or surrounded by strangers. This wasn't my Nara.

"People change, Fabian. But I changed too much. Meeting Captain Echo was the point where I knew I would never be welcomed here again. I held out as long as I could because… because I couldn't bear to leave you behind." She sniffed and forced a smile, crushing with those next five words as Captain Echo reappeared, howling as the trees swayed heavily in the wind, "You are my everything, Fabian."

I didn't know what else to do. I was 12 years old, and this was uncharted territory for anyone. I pulled her into a hug and told her I'd miss her. What else was I going to do? It's not like I could fight the Captain, and I didn't want to upset her more than she already was. We held each other for what felt like an eternity, before she pulled away and kissed me once, wiping a tear away before taking Captain Echo's hand and walking into the darkness as I sat there, crying. I waited for hours for her to come back, but she never did.

Defeated, I walked home, and no sooner had I got through the door, my mom pulled me into a tight hug, sobbing.

"Oh, my sweet boy, are you okay!? Where have you been?!" She was holding me so tightly, and while I'm sure my crying had set off alarm bells, this was still a bit much.

"Ma, I was in the haven with Nara… we were…" I began, before a voice behind my mom cut me off.

"Where is she now, Fabian? Why isn't she here with you?" It was an older man in his late 40s, smartly dressed and oozing with authority. The kind of guy you knew wouldn't have an issue with raising a hand to you if you stepped out of line. Nara's father. "I swear if that stupid girl has gone off exploring again… she will regret it."

"She's gone, Mr Anisha." I said, flatly. Mr Anisha summarily broke the calm that was in the home, grabbing me and shaking me as he screamed for her whereabouts, my mom pulling him off of me.

"She went into the woods. She said I couldn't follow her. She said she belonged there." I said, emotions now rushing through me as I raised my voice at him. "What was I supposed to do?!"

"Be a man and go after her. She's your best friend, isn't she? Or are you just like every other boy going after my stupid daughter? She's gotten herself into this mess, but YOU should have protected her instead of being a spineless coward! If my daughter is hurt in any way…" He reared forward again, fist shaking as my mother screamed at him to calm down or that she'd call the police.

"SHE'S NOT ALONE."

The room fell deathly silent. Both my mom and Mr. Anisha stared at me.

"She's with our friend. I thought he wasn't real, but I met him… he's harmless, I swear!" I felt desperation overtaking me as their faces fell from shock to abject horror. "His name is Captain Echo, he's a spirit of the woods and he—"

I didn't get to say any more than that. My mom ushered me up to my room and told me to stay in there until she came back, no matter what. Over the next few hours, I'd hear angry voices, crying, screaming, and a lot of chatter from people I didn't know coming and going. She came back the next day and told me I had to answer some questions, but that it would never be spoken of again afterwards. I protested, but she shot me a glance full of such terror that I dared not challenge it.

The next few months were a blur, I was out of school for a while and even when I was there, I didn't pay attention to the teachers who looked at me with a mixture of concern and disgust, the kids who hid from me like the plague as I was "the one who got Naya killed" and the world felt bleaker for it. I stayed in my room, the days blurring together until I just stopped checking altogether.

It was eventually decided I needed a fresh start, so I was moved out of state to be with my relatives before I started the next school year. It took some adjusting but, ultimately, it was the best thing imaginable for my mental health. The events of that summer, though painful, became easier to deal with and I could move past them.

At the beginning of the year, I decided to go back and visit my family for a few months. I'd lived with my aunt and uncle for most of my teenage years and I relished the time I got to spend with my mom. While it was nice, and we reminisced about my childhood, it naturally didn't take long for the subject of that night to be brought up and now, as adults, discussed.

"Do you remember what Naya called the thing in the woods?" She asked me, a glass of wine in a shaking hand. I nodded.

"Yeah, she said his name was Captain Echo, didn't know where it came from but that it just appeared in her mind."

Mom shook her head, biting her lip.

"Honey, the area you explored as kids is called Echo Forests, because the farther you got in, the more your voice would carry from so many directions. It was a great hiding spot, and you could practically go in there undetected. Nara never came up with that name. It was already there. She had a phenomenal mind for creativity, but that one wasn't on her."

I stared at her, dumbstruck. "But… what about the Captain part, the way he looked and all the things he showed us?"

She finished her wine with a swig and pulled out a newspaper clipping from the 1980s, sliding it over to me. The attached photo was of a small boy sitting on a set of steps on an old church porch, smiling at the cameraman. The headline next to it read:

### "YOUNG ARTIST, 10, VANISHES. LAST SEEN ENTERING ECHO FOREST."

I clutched it, eyes reading it over and over again as my mom put a hand on my shoulder and carried on talking.

"You probably heard about it growing up, but there is an urban legend of a boy who went missing by the old church and that he haunts the building. This is that young boy, he was a genius painter and right as he was getting attention, he vanished into the woods with someone." She sighed. I refused to take my eyes off of the photo. "Nara was also a gifted painter who vanished into the woods with someone, but it wasn't a forest spirit, it wasn't a goblin, and it wasn't something otherworldly, honey… It was a man. A very, very sick man."

No, she was right, I'd pretended for so long that he was a forest spirit or a friendly entity, that I didn't notice the way his hands ran through Nara's hair, how he told us about a magical place deep in the woods where we could stay forever and Nara could be free of her cruel father, the strange foods in the forest he'd force us to eat so we'd lose track of time and consciousness. I pushed it all down in my mind and convinced myself he was something more.

"Did… did they find him? Or Nara?" I croaked, my mind rushing with thoughts as uncomfortable truths came to the surface. Mom shook her head. "Then how the hell can you know all this?!" I cried. She gave me the kind of motherly smile that conveyed so much pain and pity in one single moment.

"You were so alone after she went missing, all you did was sit by your window and look at the forest. You wouldn't eat, wouldn't sleep, just sat there night after night drawing in the sketchbook Nara left behind. You refused to let anyone touch it. But when you finally passed out, I looked and saw you'd drawn that… thing staring into your bedroom night after night, sometimes with Nara and sometimes not. I decided there and then we'd move you out and give you the life she couldn't have." She held my hands in hers, tears running down her face. "We couldn't save her, but I could save you, baby."

I hugged her, overwhelmed by all of this and not sure what to make of it. I told her I was going to bed and that I'd talk to her in the morning, but sleep eluded me, and I decided documenting this for others may be worthwhile. Because if I'd just believed her when she said she had an imaginary friend that was only in her mind, maybe she wouldn't have stumbled across Captain Echo. Maybe we would've been together, and that sick fuck may have lost a victim he wanted to capture.

Or maybe, just maybe, there's something lurking in our forests, in our seas, our mountains. Ancient, unknown things we may stumble upon one day and decide how to respond. Nara chose acceptance while I ran.

All I know now, is as I finish my thoughts and put an end to this, my old bedroom window is open and I can remember why the forests have their name, why I'm venturing out there tonight to find the truth in all of this,

I can hear the howling of the Captain calling out to me.

And now my mind turns to the ritual we used to use for the ghost by the church, the bow and the affirmation. My mind lingers on Nara for a moment before bowing and getting ready to head out,

I see you. I acknowledge you. I remember you.

# THE FAMILY TRADITION

On the 30th of August, at around 7:15pm… I turned 30.

Our family, the Lea's, has always been seen as eccentric by the locals. Some of us have become inventors, artisans, masters of niche crafts and the like. We've lived full, happy, and creatively stimulating lives, seen to the outside world as to not have a care in the world or need for anything.

But we have this life at a great cost.

A ritual that must be undertaken every August 30th. Known collectively as *The Waiting Ritual.*

My family has had this tradition for over 250 years. Every member of the family above the age of 18 congregates at my family's estate and spends the 48 hours prior to the "event" catching up, partying and generally enjoying themselves.

They are, after all, all living on borrowed time.

When the final hours tick down to the event, they detox, ensure they've slept well, done their business and have plenty to hydrate. Because once the clock strikes midnight, they must all stay in one room until the clock again strikes midnight.

The entire time, they must keep at least one other family member in eyeshot. No single member of the family must be unaccounted for.

The parlour room is structured in such a way that we can see each other no matter where we are situated in the room. Each area is well-lit, comfortable, and accommodating. Which, when you deal with roughly 30 people, is a necessity.

You have to understand, growing up in this environment had me thinking this was simply a normal tradition every family undertook. I saw no strangeness in spending my birthdays away from my family members, that it was just "bad luck" my birthday fell on the traditional day.

That, of course, would change after I turned 11.

I remember the first time I learned of *The Waiting Ritual*, my mother was supposed to host my birthday party but apologised and said she wouldn't be home in time from work. To that point in my life, Mom had always worked long hours to provide for us, and it was routine. I was crestfallen, but I understood. She was an art curator and loved her job with an unbridled passion, she was my hero. The fact we shared a birthday only made our bond more special in my eyes. She was a best friend as well as my mom… and I don't know a lot of kids who can say that.

I still remember the smell of lavender in her hair, the way her eyes flickered and the way she hugged me tight before saying goodbye.

"Never forget how special you are, Theo. The fact you're here is nothing short of a miracle, and that is worth celebrating. I love you." She kissed me on the forehead and promised us pizza when she got home to make up for it. I remember the babysitter waving her off as I got the house ready for my friends so we could play Nintendo and stay up late, but something in the pit of my stomach was uneasy… like I'd missed the step up on the stairs.

When Mom didn't come home the following day, that feeling blossomed, sprouted wings and flew into my heart, where it started breaking away at the fragile casing until it would shatter spectacularly.

There was no funeral. The police seemed disinterested in finding her and my family said very little about it to me, just that "she'd gone away" and that I'd understand when I was older.

I was a day away from turning 18 when my Great Uncle Thaddeus told me I had to come to the family estate for my birthday, that it was "time". I remember being pissed because I had a date with my high school crush, but that was of little interest to him and saying no wasn't a wise idea, so I gave in.

We drove in relative silence for the majority of the journey. He kept his steely eyed gaze on the road and furrowed his brow. The man was in his 70s but still commanded a room with his gait. I tried to block out the feelings of teenage frustration and focus on the country road.

"We miss Kristina too, you know." He grumbled from behind a thick white moustache. "Your mum was a wonderful woman.

Beautiful soul and a vision of the world like nothing I'd seen before. But with her and your Aunt Cecilia now gone… Well, it's a good thing you're turning 18." He drummed his fingers against the wheel, I said nothing and instead chose to let my feelings swirl around inside of me as we pulled up on the Lea estate.

A secluded manor house in the countryside, it had sat here for nearly 3 centuries with upkeep repairs in various areas, but largely remained the same grandiose spectacle of architecture it'd been when first constructed. All members of the Lea family were born here, me included. It was a rite of passage, in a way.

As we headed inside, the remnants of the party from Friday night still scattered around, a very sombre atmosphere greeted me in the parlour room.

Spread out amongst bean bag chairs, leather couches, armchairs and ottomans were the entire adult Lea clan members. Among them were my Great Aunt Agnes, Uncle George, Aunt Liza, Cousin's Mick and Ralph… and sat in a large chair at the back was my grandpa, Sir Walter Quincy Carter Lea, a distinguished man with a usually jovial spirit, but now sat morose and deflated, as if carrying the weight of the world on his shoulders.

His eyes never left mine as I awkwardly shuffled into the room. In fact, none of theirs did. 30 pairs of eyes fixated on me as I sat opposite Walter and gave him a half-hearted smile.

"Theodore, I'm sure you're wondering why you're here. And since you're a man now, I will not sugar-coat it." Walter's voice broke the silence and, much like his facial expression, it was dripping in weariness. "The Lea family has been blessed with fortune, fame, and success in all things. We have had this for a very, very long time. But it comes at a cost. We have a… contract, of sorts, that must be fulfilled on August 30th. Every year, without fail."

He slid across an old, dried-up piece of parchment with a slew of signatures and requirements. I scanned it and felt all the moisture leave my mouth.

*On this day in 1756, I, Theodore James Wellington Lea, patriarch of the Lea family, do hereby commit our earthly bodies and eternal souls to undertake this practice until we are either no more, or our obligation is deemed fulfilled.*

*Starting in the waning days of August, we shall congregate on these grounds and be merry, cavort and enjoy our lives as one is wanton to do.*

*But as the clock strikes midnight and hails on the 30th day of the month, we shall undertake* The Waiting Ritual *and obey these basic tenements as set out and agreed upon by both parties:*

*1: All members of the Lea family over the age of 18 must be present.*

*2: All members of the Lea family must keep at least one other member in sight at all times.*

*3: If there is a designated 'focus' of the Lea family, they are to be stared at constantly.*

*4: Should any members of the Lea family hear voices that distract them, they are to ignore them.*

*5: Lights must be available at all times, including back-up matches, should there be an issue.*

*6: Line of sight must not be broken until the clock once again chimes 12 times to usher in August 31st.*

*I do sign my name in blood to signify the commitment to this pact and the promise that current and future generations of the Lea family shall continue this practice, lest we invoke the consequences of non-completion.*

*Signed: Theodore James Wellington Lea*
*Witness: Elnora Mica Lea (Spouse)*

In place of the alternate signature was a bizarre series of characters that I had never seen before. I'd half expected the devil himself to have put his name down, but this just made me feel uncomfortable.

"What the hell is this? An elaborate birthday prank?" I tried to force a laugh, but my body wouldn't cooperate. Grandpa Walter shook his head.

"No, lad, it's a commitment to the agreement. Your mother was our original focus person and now that you're of age, it's you. All you must do is sit in the chair and wait it out for 24 hours.

We will be here with you. When the time is up, you can go. Your successes will come to you naturally and life will be plentiful." He gestured to the room around him. "All of us have had great lives and our children, your cousins, will continue this trend. Provided we do our part here and now."

What choice did I have? I agreed and Grandpa presented me with a different document that every member of the family had signed in blood on their 18th birthday. I did the same and was free to talk to everyone before the clock chimed midnight.

Once it had, we all took our seats, and the ritual began.

I won't lie. It was initially still feeling like a prank that I was waiting on for the rug to be pulled out from under me. But as the first hour passed and conversation grew sparse, I realised how seriously everyone was taking this.

Imagine being sat in a chair at the back of a grand parlour, books strewn across you from side to side, the well-lit room full of your family members. Some you get on well with, others you avoid like the plague.

And every single one of them is staring at you. Incessantly. For 24 hours.

About halfway through, still during the day, things would become less tense. Something about the daylight brought with it a comfort of visibility that could not be taken away and conversations grew lively again.

By the time we reached 10:30pm, however, tensions were high. Darkness had enveloped the room and one of my aunts explained that this is when things can go wrong, but stopped herself from continuing any further, hands shaking.

I would hear faint whispers from outside in the hall that I brushed off as the maid or a younger family member conversing, but could never totally remove from my mind. The lights would flicker, and everyone seemed to be on edge.

But we made it to midnight and, on that final chime, the group erupted into cheers and congratulations to one another; me included. It felt like we'd just come up for air for the first time in decades. Life tasted fresh, and all we wanted to do was experience it.

A small and short party was had as thanks, but we were all admittedly so tired that it didn't get too far. I would bow out before 3am and sleep through the rest of the 31st, going about my life as normal as possible from that day on.

Grandpa was right. My life found great success with each passing year. I would be accepted to the art school I had as my top pick. I became a recognised artist and people all over the world knew of my work. A family of my own may have eluded me, but I was a happy 29-year-old for all things considered, even if my partner resented my birthday ritual.

I hadn't explained it to her yet and didn't have plans to do so for as long as possible.

Outsiders never fully understood, and it wasn't permitted to have anyone not married involved. I liked Harriet a lot, but I was not ready to go down that route any time soon.

She gave me a defeated goodbye as I left. This was the 2nd birthday of mine she'd gotten to be a part of, and it was clearly bothering her that she couldn't indulge me in the way she wanted. I told her we'd have all the time afterwards, but this did little to assuage her frustrations.

"You always keep secrets, Theo. I don't like it." She huffed, understandably frustrated at not being let in. "How can we progress with our relationship if you keep me at arm's length? You've not even told me about your mother, and it's been nearly 2 years."

"I wish I knew myself, but that's just how it is." I shrugged. This was something that hurt, but I'd had many years to process. "And if we ever get married, you'll learn all about what goes on, okay?"

The simple prospect of even mentioning marriage put a smile on her face and she seemed to forget all about her frustrations. She kissed me and sent me off without a second thought.

The Lea Estate, by this point, was largely a mix of old and new members. Cousins Mitchell, Eric, Sadie, Pippa, and Kiefer had all long since turned 18 and were now successful 20-something's, my aunts and uncles from years prior still able to come along.

Surprisingly, my grandpa was still the active patriarch. Even at 87, he had plenty of vigour and was relieved to see me pull up, ready to undertake the festivities and party. Now that I'd been doing this for 12 years, it had become a macabre routine that we loved and hated in equal measure. We ate, drank, talked about life and love. We existed and made sure to cherish those moments.

Then, as the clock struck midnight, we took our places and that familiar chill washed over all of us.

I don't know what was different. Thinking about it now, something had to have been off, but when you're in a routine for so long, even an odd one like ours can begin to feel mundane.

We locked all the doors, entered the parlour, took our seats and so it began.

The first 30 minutes was of no real issue, some idle chatter here and there, but largely everyone was steeling themselves for the long day ahead. Cousin Mick was using a stress ball whilst Cousin Ralph had a single earphone in with an audiobook on his phone. Smart decision.

At 12:35am, there was a smash against the window. It sounded as if a bird had flown headfirst into the glass, intent on crushing itself. We jumped, but years of experience didn't have us all staring at the window. Instead, Pippa went over within our line of sight and opened the curtains.

A cracked window, but no bird. In the distance, we could see something moving, but it wasn't possible to figure out without closer inspection… and that wasn't possible. The family estate is a private land that borders on a large, wooded area. We don't govern that part of the land and instead have large fences around the property that show where our ownership begins.

So why would anyone be willingly out there?

"Shits weird, right?" I chuckled, looking at my grandpa and expecting a nervous laugh back.

Instead, he shook in his chair and kept his gaze on me, sweat pouring down his nose and his skin growing sallow.

"It's just like last time, with Kristina…" he breathed. "We tried to cheat the system and we're still paying for it…"

Cheat the system? What the hell was he talking about?

I scanned the room and the older members of the family looked increasingly agitated and anxious, my Aunt Gertrude bordering on hysterical as she whispered something to my uncle Bill, pointing a shaking finger at me. He would calm her, and we'd spend the next 2 hours in almost total silence.

But when the lights began to flicker, and the anxiety rose again, I felt myself needing to ask, "What's going on, Grandpa?" I breathed, the tension spreading through the group like a disease. He shifted uncomfortably, and my concern only grew. "If you don't tell me right now, I'll walk out of this building and that'll be the end of the tradition."

He immediately leapt out of his seat, eyes wide and wild.

"No, absolutely not! We do not need any more suffering and death in this family!"

The room grew cold and my blood along with it.

"Death? Mum… died?" The sheer pain of those words leaving my body like the very air was being pulled from my lungs by force. He sank back into his chair, defeated.

"This deal we made… It granted us everything we could want, but there is no deal in this world without a price. That price was for one of us to fail the contract's requirements each year." There was a tension in the air, permeating through every member of the family as he spoke. "The contract never originally stipulated we all must gather together, in fact it actively persuaded us to "elect" someone to miss the proceedings, to perhaps never inform them of the deal. The trick set out was to do it on a day that would keep at least one of us apart. We would have obstacles from life or employment that would ensure at least one of us would be unable to make it each year, thus fulfilling their end of the bargain. I don't remember who came up with the idea, but your grandmother… My wife was in heavy labour when your mother was due and the family wanted to be there. It just seemed like we'd been thrown a line… no more death. So, we decided to make it a mandatory rite of passage for the family. By some stroke of luck, your mother was born just after the stroke of midnight on the 30th and you in the early evening on the 30th some 25 years later. For over half a century, we were able to maintain peace and tranquillity." His lip quivered, and the lights flickered again. "But all debts must be repaid, especially with them…"

In a brief moment, for a fraction of a second, I saw something stand in the middle of our parlour. It towered over all of us, hunched over with its bulbous head against the ceiling, red eyes fixated on me. If there was a mouth, I couldn't see it. It held up a twisted digit to its face as if to shush me before the lights flickered back on.

If Grandpa or anyone else saw it, they didn't acknowledge it. I tried my best to hold my nerve and ask a question to keep my focus.

"What are they?" I managed to muster, hoping there'd be some kind of explanation for what I saw. Maybe an old legend I could connect to them to make sense of all this.

But Grandpa just looked at me, a single tear running down his face as the proud patriarch of our family showed true fear for the first time in my life:

"I don't know. Nobody does. They appeared to our ancestor, your namesake, so long ago. He said at the time they were a spectre from beneath the Earth. His wife insisted they came from the stars. His son was adamant they were an old Celtic legend forgotten to time. But nobody has ever truly known. But we do know one thing, Theo."

The entire family came together, held hands, and softly hummed as they stared at me, trying to fight the fear:

"When we break eye contact… when we don't fulfil our part of the bargain, bad things happen."

I heard more whispering outside, the sounds of walls being knocked upon, and something unseen and gargantuan thundering around the home.

It was trying to get our attention.

"Is that what happened to Mum? Did someone in this room fail to fulfil their part of the bargain?" I felt a hot rage and grief push their way up, compounded by that feeling of being upset on my birthday of all days. I looked around and my eyes settled on Aunt Gertrude, the most nervous of the bunch. She was my last auntie and Kristina's eldest sister. "What did you do, Auntie?"

She pursed her lips, and I could see the veins in her temple throbbing, trying desperately to hold her composure. But the noises were unrelenting and nobody in the room was attempting to calm her, as if they knew this needed to happen.

"I… always resented your mother, Theodore. She was pretty, confident, young, and full of energy. Always got the recognition from Father, the love she wanted and the life she sought. I was never satisfied with what I had… and I thought if she was gone… maybe that good fortune would shine on me? So, I took some sleeping pills and passed out…" The staring felt malicious, angry, full of spite and a hint of regret. "I don't have any ill will towards you, Theodore. But if it meant I could live the life I have now, I'd do it again."

"Bitch," Pippa and Sadie piped up from the sides. Both of them loved their Aunt Kristina.

"All of you knew, huh? Never told him? Were you even planning to?" Kiefer spat on the floor in disgust. "This family should fucking burn."

I felt my head swell, a cocktail of emotions coupled with the unseen attempts to distract us.

Grandpa took my shoulders in both hands and looked at me, the saddest smile I'd ever seen on a person's face.

"I let the smartest and most talented of my girls go because of tradition. Rest assured, I won't do it to you. We've seen enough death and enough loss in this family. Before your mother's birth, we would see two dozen of our family taken in as many years. She stabilised us, you continued that. But keeping this from you was the wrong decision, especially at your age…" He let go, backing up to the parlour door. "So, if you want to leave, to confront whatever takes us, to get your revenge on us… we won't stop you."

The family murmured but didn't protest. Gertrude sobbed silently.

"How do I know it won't take me?" My legs shook as I stood up. It was barely 3am by this point, we had so long to go.

"You don't. But that is part of you making the choice, instead of us. Perhaps if you are the one to leave, it will punish us instead?"

I stood there for a few minutes, deciding over my choices. How to respond to a family steeped in secrecy that would willingly send my mother and I to slaughter in order to keep proliferating.

It turned out I wouldn't need to wait very long for a decision.

The front door hadn't been properly locked, and Harriet came in, blasting music and armed with a mobile strobe lighting machine. I'd told her that while we had a ritual, I'd focused instead on the partying aspect.

She followed me here.

The second she entered the house, pumping music and the lights shining through the room, they hit several of the family members in the face, breaking eye contact.

And just like that, the pact was broken.

I don't know if I can fully articulate what happened, but I felt a deep rumble beneath my feet.

The air grew thick, and it felt as if time had slowed down.

Something was stirring and as I looked around at the family… I could see on their faces they knew it was coming for them.

I looked at Grandpa, still smiling and nodding as the lights went out.

I made a direct beeline out of the room with Harriet in hand, slamming the parlour door behind me and pushing my body weight up against it.

"What the fuck is going on, Theo?" She screamed, confused and distressed.

"You just killed us all. All because you couldn't wait… you… you…"

I tried to find the words. To find the rage… But I was beyond that. I held her close, and we kept our heads down, hoping to make it through whatever hell was behind just a few inches of wood.

I saw nothing. But I heard everything.

A cacophony of shrill voices screaming, laughing, singing and groaning in one torrent of suffering. Things were thrown around the room. Possibly furniture, possibly a body.

I sat against that fucking door until daybreak this morning, when Cousin Pippa gently knocked against the door and told us to come in. That it "didn't matter this year anymore".

Opening the door, I saw carnage. The room was singed black from wall to wall. Most of the family were lying face down or cowering in the corner, completely unresponsive.

As I scanned the room, wordless, full of anxiety and trepidation, I already knew who would be missing:

Grandpa.

No trace of him existed, as if he'd been wiped from existence.

But, to my surprise, Gertrude had been taken, too. A smear of blood next to her husband that ran across the length of the wall and ended in the corner. Her husband simply rocked back and forth, holding her green shawl.

My attention was then drawn to the centre of the room, to something I took with me to the car. Something I have in front of me now that the full 24 hours have passed, and I have 364 days to decide on what to do next.

The family went home, all of us fully understanding what had transpired. Harriet tried in vain to apologise to them, but each one treated her as if she was a ghost.

After all, she wasn't part of the family. She wasn't part of the ritual. A part of the game. For all that I'd learned, I still didn't know what they were or where Mom and Grandpa had gone.

I dropped Harriet home and made her swear to never talk about it. She was devastated but understood. When she asked me what I intended to do, I simply shook my head.

The contract had been amended, you see. Not that there's anything anyone here can do about it aside from listening. To know these things happen.

The Waiting Ritual had been extended to 48 hours. All must attend. Graver consequences for those who don't.

A simple note written in obsidian ink had been pinned to the top. Gertrude's signature crossed out and Harriet's name written in her place.

"A trade. A new debt. Two more next year."

# THE INNER VOICE

I used to think everyone had an inner voice. A little disembodied narrator that, when unfocused, sounded familiar yet not. But something we could take from our own voice and turn into that of a celebrity, a cartoon character or whatever we wished.

So, it was a shock when I found out that it's likely a third of the population has no idea what that is like. No guiding voice through their actions, reminding them of the tasks for the day or even helping them run through problems in their mind.

Nothing. Just blissful silence. Or maybe agonising, depending on who you talk to.

My inner voice was always prominent as I grew up. I don't recall the shape or tone of it as a child, just that it was a good confidant when things got rough. If my dad came home drunk and decided to take his anger out on my mom, my inner voice would advise me of the safest places to hide and tell me stories or replay songs to cover up the horrible sounds.

The voice would soothe me in bed as I healed, sobbing into my pillow as my father stormed out to "get some air", usually only returning days later in a trancelike state.

Being an only child, I spent a lot of my time either playing make-believe in my room with my Transformers and Lego, traversing fantastical worlds on my DreamCast or exploring the vast fields that surrounded our little village of Minoesha, just next to Mantis Bay. There weren't many families around and my folks were isolationists, said that Sturgeons big cities had plenty of evil within them, that their god wasn't the right god and if we wanted to eke out a safe living, it'd be here, off the land.

My inner voice would always warn me not to go to the Coyle family plot that bordered on Minoesha and the nearby woods. I remember this was the first instance where I could recall the shape and rhythm of the voice inside me. Cool, collected, mystifying.

**"It's too far, and your parents will get mad. We don't want that. Besides…"**

A strong wind blew from the depths of the woods and rattled the rotted wooden foundations, threatening to unearth secrets buried in the soil.

**"Great tragedy will befall the next person to go into those woods."**

It sounded almost sombre, melancholy in its tone. Amid the rationalisation in my own mind, this voice stood out and felt like it was urging me in its own way to take those tentative steps back and away from the family plot.

But someone else in the town lacked the same kind of voice I had.

And it was the first time I got scared of it.

Micah Duponse was a very outgoing kid, and this being the 90s, was given a lot more freedom to do so than nowadays. Parents either weren't as aware of the dangers in rural communities or they simply didn't pay as much attention. Micah had decided that he was going to venture beyond the borders and go near the Coyle plot, knowing full well that all of us in Minoesha were told repeatedly to avoid it.

The alarm was raised some 6 hours later when the lights came on and Micah was nowhere to be seen.

3 days later, Micah's body was discovered within the run-down shack. He'd been strung upside down on a hook like a slab of meat and, if the rumours were true, had been partially feasted upon before discovery by the authorities.

I remember the moments following the discovery, in the deafening silence between breaths and feigned apologies to the community for not doing a better job of safeguarding their young against unseen dangers. My inner voice chimed in, **"I told you it wasn't a good idea. Now, let's see how close to the bone this will end up being…"**

I tried to formulate the question in my mind to ask the voice, picturing a puzzled look and even a question mark, but it yielded nothing of merit, save for a coy response.

**"You'll see."**

My dad began to act more reserved, cagey in his behaviour. He ate meals on his own, loud slurps from his soup bowl and bloodshot eyes darting to every exit our house had. No more beatings, berating, or nighttime trips.

It was a couple of days later when my inner voice woke me up out of bed, the kind of loud noise that snaps you awake but without the clarity to understand what happened.

**"Go for a walk. You need the fresh air."**

I blinked, eyes still heavy from tiredness and the desire to put my head on the pillow overwhelming. I began to rest back down when the voice rang out again, this time from the corner of my room. **"You really do need the fresh air, Sunny."**

I felt a primal sense of fear that I can only equate to being in a tiger pit or any small space with a creature you have no business being so close to. I wasn't able to make out any features in the corner, no terrifying aspects to burn into my mind or send my fear to new heights. It was entirely obscured, but I knew it was there. Watching me.

**"Get out of bed and climb down the tree by your window and go for a walk, Sunny. Go until I tell you to come back."**

I obeyed, still young enough to respect an authoritative voice and one that admittedly had proven itself on a handful of occasions. I grabbed some sturdy clothing and did as instructed, walking around the block and keeping to the streetlights, enjoying the cool air on my face.

For about a half hour, each time I rounded the corner to go back, the voice would softly tell me.

**"No, not yet, Sunny. One more walk should do it. If you go back now, your path will change."**

On the fourth rotation, I ignored the voice, and my sleepy body was beginning to overpower my urge to listen. I turned the corner and saw flashing lights emanating from my house. Surely, I'd not been gone too long for them to call the police? 40 minutes at the very most?

Figuring out what I'd say as an excuse, I started to tentatively walk closer to the front of the house when I realised what I was seeing.

Officers taking up positions by their open car doors, firearms trained on the front of the property, focused and ready to fire.

Following their line of sight, I saw my father's crazed and weather-beaten form clutching my mother with a pistol to her temple, ranting and raving about how he knew this was going to happen, that they'd never find him where he was going.

"Mr. Wimslow, this doesn't need to end in bloodshed. We can settle this peacefully, nobody else needs to suffer if you cooperate…"

Nobody else? What did he…

As I got closer, Dad saw me and took a step back, glancing up at the room I'd been in, mumbling to himself.

In that momentary lapse, Mom tried to push free, setting off the gun and a shot to her skull. She fell, eyes open and staring at me as blood pooled around her.

Time slowed. Dad stared down at her, arms still in their position, and said something under his breath before pointing the gun at me, smiling.

In an instant, he was gunned down by the officers and fell backwards through the screen door, twitching and mumbling as I was pulled away by officers, still screaming. The only sound left in my ears was that of the internal monologue, trying to calm me.

**"I warned you not to go back, Sunny."**

*******

Dad would eventually be charged with the murder of Micah and several other missing persons, including that of the Coyle family some decade and a half ago. I'll stop short of saying my dad was a serial killer, but he was categorically a fucking monster. In the sole appointment he had with a psychiatrist, months before he got caught, he was talking about how he never felt himself when angry. Said that it was as if something overtook him and compelled him to do bad things, that he was still aware, but barely. When he finished these fits of rage and had control, he'd go out to the Coyle estate and meditate, try to home in on the rage and control it.

He said it was here that something bad happened, and that he fed on this energy… made him stronger. I don't know what the fuck he was talking about.

The Minoeshan Massacre was what they called it, a colourful name for an ugly man and one I was happy to be rid of, even if I did miss my mom.

The voice went silent after that for several years. I grew up, found a good foster home, and settled into my life, going through high school with aspirations of becoming a journalist, looking at the truth behind what went on around this strange town.

It was on my 27th birthday that the voice came back, but with a very different intonation. I was walking through Sturgeon's entertainment district when it commanded me in my head with the force of a thunderclap:

**"STOP."**

You never realise how powerful social cues are until you hear someone say something like that or see someone gesture you to slow down when running. I did as it instructed and stood by an alleyway between two buildings: a cabaret club on the left and an arcade to the right.

**"Do you know what's down there, Sunny?"**

The voice called out, a degree of foreboding rippling through its voice. It knew something I didn't... but how the hell is that even possible?

Something rustles in the darkness, not far from a dumpster situated next to the cabaret club's back door. A pile of thick, fetid garbage bags starts crinkling as something pushes up against them.

The penny hasn't dropped yet.

I gazed down the stretch of wonderment and bright lights, chemistry in my brain doing its best to fire up the neutrons and make an astute guess, but the voice got there first.

The penny hangs in the air, spinning on its axis and my goosebumps bubbling to the surface like insects trying to dig their way free before bad luck befalls them too.

**"There is a special place people find themselves when making a critical choice. They stay a while, tell a story, and have a drink, getting their answer..."** it pauses, as if mulling over its next choice of words carefully. I feel something crawl on my back. **"But you need not venture down there, your path lies elsewhere. After all..."**

A lumbering shape wrenches itself free from the garbage pile. A crooked limb with a malformed, greying hand drags a tall corpse free from the clutches of waste. It cracks as it stands to its full height and stands looking away from me, hiding its face behind long, spindly fingers.

The penny drops as the voice keeps talking, no longer isolated to my head, but still ringing inside my skull as the figure speaks. It's as if I have the same dialogue playing from two sources.

**"Your destiny is already set in stone, just as your fathers was."**

I stumble back, tripping over myself and falling to the ground with a thud, heart slamming against my ribcage. What the fuck did he mean by that?

Not a single bit of dialogue exchanged on my end, yet he was able to communicate with me freely… was this all in my head? Or was it…

**"Something more? Yes, Sunny. You're not going doo-lally, I was just waiting for you to… mature. Come, I'll show you. Cast your eyes across the street to the woman by the bus stop… the pretty thing looking anxious and frail. Red dress."**

Again, social cues being what they are, I did as instructed. Sure enough, a young woman paced back and forth by the bus stop, her makeup running down her face and glasses fogged up from the stress. She was a larger woman, carrying such grace and beauty about her, the red and white polka-dot dress flowing in the soft breeze. But her form was anything but that.

**"She is going to make a decision that will change the course of four lives. You will beat a man to death as a result of that decision. Watch."** The voice called. It was pragmatic, calculated. As if reading the weather report for the next few days. Cloudy with a strong indication of violence.

I didn't take my eyes off of her as a loud, brutish man began bellowing from the bottom of the street, hailing expletives at her without a care or concern for the people around.

"Sadie! There you are! You stupid fat bitch, the fuck you think you're doing? Going out without my say so… I oughta smack you down right here, right now!" His eyes were bloodshot, speech slurred, fists balled into cinderblocks. Every step he took bore malicious intent, each limb ready to enact untold damage. The woman, Sadie, locked eyes with him and bit her lip to the point of drawing blood.

It was then I saw the bus.

I realised what was going to happen.

I didn't think. My body acted without asking permission. I vaulted off the ground and darted across the road, desperate to get between Sadie and her partner. He was covering ground just as quickly as the bus, implausibly so. I could see her gaze focus longingly on the road, the escape from it all and the opportunity the bus provided… but I was determined.

I caught up behind the man and Sadie, shoving him out of the way in order to stop her from doing anything, grabbing her by the shoulders and looking her dead in the eyes, panic-stricken across them.

"It's alright, I heard him from across the street, you're safe now." I flashed a grin and tried to find other words of comfort, but that panicked gaze wasn't aimed at me.

It was frozen in horror at the road.

"Neil…" she breathed, just as an ear-splitting scream cut the air and was followed by the sound of a horn blaring, a thud, and bones splitting under the force of the bus's wheels.

She pushed me aside and ran to the bus, hollering and sobbing uncontrollably. I simply stood and stared straight ahead, unable and unwilling to look at the carnage I'd just enacted.

**"Do you believe me now, Sunny?"**

The voice was behind me, long hands on my shoulders pushing me forward ever so slightly, as if guiding me.

What just happened?

**"I'm a gift, Sunny. I'm the sort of thing that most never hear about beyond furtive whispers, in fairytales or at large family gatherings, when the matriarch has had one too many. I'm a parasite, of sorts, that came with you as a package deal… as did all my kin in your family bloodline. We guide you, lead you down a path that best serves us and feeds us, helps our next generation grow even stronger."** He leads me down a side alley and my pace picks up. I feel my body become less under my control as I slide under one fence and hop over another, muscles performing far beyond what my average self should be able to achieve.

Before long, I'm sprinting through the back alleys of Sturgeon, deep into the slums of the entertainment district and in the heart of the concrete jungle. The hands that were on my shoulder now controlling me like a puppet, leading me somewhere.

"What… what happened with…" I try to talk between breaths, just to make sure I could still do so. The voice chuckles but doesn't stop my movements. I pass the grand Hotel Inertia and make a turn into a storm drain.

**"Your Father? He was weak willed. The voice, my father, spoke to him early on and he gave into the whispers far too easily. Made assimilation no problem at all by the time he was a grown man… It was through this overindulgence that I sought to protect you, Sunny. Something I still wish to do."**

"Why? If what you are feeds on negativity and bad actions, then aren't I just going to end up the same way?!" I grit my teeth and tense my muscles, agony spreading through my body as I resist, halting my pace and smacking into a wall I refused to turn away from before I could stop. My face crunches with the rebar and blood spurts from my nose as I groan.

**"Sunny, there is a very fine difference between assimilation and symbiosis. I wish to join with you and make you into something... more. I controlled you only to show you what we can do. I told you what would happen only to showcase what *you* can do..."**

I pull my hands from my face and see the same towering figure walk backwards towards me, feet twisted to face me, knees bent backwards and cracking with every laboured groan. It bends its back over, keeping its hands around its face as it lowers it slowly, folding its spine like a suitcase.

"Why... what is the point of this? I just killed someone because YOU showed me what would happen if I didn't!" I winced, nose gushing and fear mounting. The voice tutted.

**"I showed you what would happen because it did. That's my gift. You killed, Sunny. And with me by your side, you'll kill again. But I think you'd much rather kill for a cause than kill pointlessly, like your father did."**

It lowered down until the head was at height with my own. The sounds of thundering footsteps and yelling echoed through the entrance to the storm drain. I looked back for just a moment as I thought about my position. The voice had always guided me, spared me, saved me... would it really be so bad?

"What would you have me do?" I asked, feeling my arms regain their strength, legs feel lighter. Even when I wasn't looking, I felt its malicious smile bear down on me.

**"There will be a place to showcase your skills. To see things before they happen and act on it. You just need to trust your... inner voice. It will bring you all the luck in the world."**

People have begun entering the tunnel. Angry shouts, a gun... no, three guns trained on the darkness ahead, in my general direction... but they can't see me.

There will be repercussions. It's already too late.

"I need to know, before we continue: What are y—" I tried asking it as I turned, but coming face to face with him, unrestricted and unobscured froze me in my path. If my blood could've frozen out of my nostrils, it would have. I've tried expressing what he looks like here, but each time I go to review, it's been erased. He doesn't want me telling you their secret, how they get into your head and take over **YOUR** true inner voice until you don't know what your old inner voice was. There's so many of them out there, now. So many willing people to do things and guide them down a path. I can't resist. I have to follow his instructions now.

This is all I have left.

**"I'm The Monologue Man, Sunny."** He grinned as I took off for the darkness, already feeling the elation of violence course through my veins, snuffing out every ounce of terror as my inner voice… **MY** voice, screams for freedom in a sealed chamber.

**"And we're going to see if anyone else has an inner voice like yours."**

# AN ICEBERG THEORY... ON ME

*"The Ari Monovovich Iceberg: Explained"* 342 views, uploaded by Alexandria_Eternal 7 hours ago.

I read the title over and over, scanning for some kind of mistake in my vision. But nope, there it was staring me in the face.

How was this even a thing? Did my friends pay for some elaborate prank at my expense?

No… they'd have encouraged me to find this, and my birthday is a solid 2 months away.

Surfing YouTube late at night was, as it has been for many of my generation, a nightly coping mechanism with insomnia. I find a good, inoffensive retrospective video theory, letsplay or narration and drift off to the sultry sounds of bullshit I don't care about or gritty details of a murder. We're strange creatures, but it works.

I'd been taken by the iceberg theory videos since the memes floated around some 6 or 7 years ago, no pun intended. Now that competent YouTube personalities were dissecting the theories behind games like Super Mario 64, The Legend of Zelda and even lost media tapes made it all the more tantalising to seek them out.

But finding one about me? With my face accompanying the now foreboding iceberg photo on a stranger's channel? Yeah, not so fun anymore.

And yet I still clicked it, because of course I did.

A cold opening, no music, and a black screen for the first few seconds.

A deep, powerful voice fills my speakers. I can't tell if it's been edited or if he's simply that naturally gifted, but it makes my ear drums ring, and my hairs stand up on end.

"All good people have a degree of mystery around them. Today will be no exception. Ari Monovovich has been a fascinating individual and one that I have been eager to cover on this channel since I first came across them, I have no doubt you'll all be eager to put your thoughts in the comments below…"

The screen fades and the iceberg photo comes up in full view. I have to pause it to take in the full brevity of what I'm seeing.

For those unfamiliar, an iceberg theory video is an off shoot of an Ernest Hemmingway writing theory that the best kind of storytelling should always be under the surface, with only the tip of the iceberg poking out. A good tale gets better the further you delve into it.

It only makes sense that the same rule applies to mysteries and theories. Every popular game, tv show and everything else has conspiracy theories, dark rumours, and the like. An iceberg theory allows experts to gather the info, start from the plausible and pleasant at the top all the way down to the downright insane and, sometimes, absolutely vile.

So why had someone made one about me? An ordinary 20 something from the Midwest?

I'm not special, I've never been special. Ordinary, happy up-bringing. Ordinary, happy family.

And yet when seeing a photo of my face on the side of this iceberg, the brightness in my eyes withering away as the iceberg goes deeper, the smile growing cracked and fragile, the skin blackening… I couldn't help but press on.

The iceberg faded and the first title card came up, some soft water sounds and a gentle guitar playing as we went into the first section of the video.


## Tip of the Iceberg


I wasn't sure what to expect, if I'm honest. The video opens with some innocuous info that anyone could glean from a quick look over my Facebook or twitter posts. Nothing particularly insightful beyond my political alignment, my love of surrealist art and quotes from home stuck.

Then things began to get weird.

"Ari's favourite video game *Mass Effect* is not the one that they are most emotionally attached to. No, that honour goes to the new hit *Omori* which they have played for a staggering 200 hours and are currently on their 5th play through, seemingly doing the same thing every time and not looking for alternative endings. This was confirmed through reliable sources and their steam activity."

I looked at my gaming PC in the corner. I never streamed, I felt too uncomfortable. So many eyes watching me and judging me, asking me questions I wouldn't know how to answer.

Or didn't want to answer.

My hand traced the side of my face before recoiling and slamming into my lap in frustration.

No, now wasn't the time to think about that.

I racked my mind for these "reliable sources" and my mind could not help but go back to an odd prank my friends had pulled, coupled with the already available information through some good searching. Already cursing my public information in an age where anything and everything can be found, I resolved to watch on.

A lot of the information in the tip of the iceberg section was simply things that could be gleaned from my Facebook profile, my twitter, my TikTok and my Instagram.

"Ari's routinely blogged about their mental health and gender dysphoria, showing great solidarity in a world that is constantly changing. We also know that they would occasionally post time lapses of their struggles on TikTok and then delete them if they got too much attention. Thankfully, we saved them for research purposes."

I swallowed at that last revelation. *Research purposes.*

This was getting increasingly uncomfortable as he brought this section of the iceberg to a close.

"Ultimately, what we have here is info that is already available for consumption, and we, of course, did consume it down to the last drop. With that being said, we're upping our investigation and moving onto the next level of the iceberg."

The sound of immersing in water, bubbles floating in the blackness and the text flashed up, followed by the *Dire Dire Docks* theme from *Mario 64.*

I hated this already.

### Beneath the Surface

"Ari Monovovich was born on the 4th of May 1998 and enjoyed a constant stream of lame Star Wars jokes, but one of the prevailing and accepted theories is that they were actually born in 1997." The screen flashes a baby photo of me and a birth certificate I'd never seen before. "Documents show that Ari was not only born a year earlier, but in a completely different state."

Immediately, we were off to a disturbing start.

I felt sick. That was my full name, including my middle name that I absolutely hated. My parents, Andrei and Danica, were listed, but the DOB, state and hospital were most certainly wrong…

I felt the urge to grab my phone and call my parents, but the video carried on and I felt compelled to watch more, taking notes on my phone of anything that struck me.

"Now, we don't have full confirmation, but this is quite reliable and something we'll come back to later on in the video. But Ari suffered a debilitating injury when they were four and it required seventeen stitches. They were left with a scar, both physically and mentally. Our source says that it was caused by a—"

I paused the video and felt my eyes blur, my face burning.

No.

There's no way they could've known about that.

Mom told me the papers didn't give out a lot of info at the request of the police, said it would be damaging enough for a child my age to go through the recovery without a spotlight on me at all times.

Did she lie?

Why would she lie?

I clicked ahead; I didn't want to hear their speculations on how such an ugly thing happened to me. Therapy had done its job and if I was going to relive that, I needed to see the rest of this fucking video first.

Then maybe punch my friends square in the dick if they made this.

Or find the asshat responsible.

I grabbed a cider from the fridge and sat down with my sherpa blanket wrapped around me and my comfort animal nestled in my arms. I knew I was going to need them.

A few more bits of info passed on, things about past boyfriends and girlfriends that were relatively easy to ascertain, trips I'd enjoyed and contests I'd entered into. So far, enough to let my blood simmer down and figure out what the point of this was.

That would become far harder as we went into the next area of the iceberg.

## Bottom of the Iceberg

"As we reach the bottom of the known iceberg, it's important to look at what we truly know about Ari. They love a lot of things, security, people ringing the doorbell instead of knocking… strawberry and lime cider."

I nearly choked on the swig of my bottle. What the fuck was this? I only just got into this flavour a couple weeks ago. There's no way they could've known unless…

Oh.

Oh god.

My eyes darted to the windows, to the small convenience store just a quarter mile from my house. It was the only one within a 5-mile radius and I didn't *ever* drive to another due to fears of being away from home for too long.

They followed me.

This was not a prank by someone I knew.

Of course, that should've been obvious by now, but rationality can and will cling to the last vestiges of your fear like a stubborn child in an attempt to stop it from hurtling itself over the edge and into panic territory. A place I was firmly in now.

Gripping my stuffed animal tightly and my parents' numbers on speed-dial, I knew I had to finish this.

I had to see what more they knew.

Looking at my face in the corner, the eyes have been edited and blackened, a reddish hue hanging in the surrounding space of the photo, as if they'd tried to burn the interior of the image itself. I looked gaunt, demonic and my happy smile was twisted into something I barely recognised.

Again, the slow, deep voice spoke.

"There's a theory that Ari is extremely private about their home life and living situation, to the point that they have a job that requires no face-to-face interaction and a home with nearly a dozen unique locks. I can confirm that this is, in fact, true and is due in part to Ari's desire to escape from the person they once were. While I don't think it'd be right for me to say WHO they once were, they're trying in vain, as we can never avoid who we once were or our responsibilities to that old life."

There was a pause as photos of me from my social media were put up on the screen, old school photos of me hanging out with friends, sleepovers, and gaming nights. I looked so happy…

"Ari's comfort animal smells like peppermint."

I froze. Staring at the screen as a photo of Artemis, my comfort stuffed animal, flashed up and was accompanied by a photo of me sleeping.

"… but contrary to popular theories, Ari instead smells like orchids."

I began hyperventilating, my hands shaking and the feeling of vomit rushing up.

This person has been in my fucking house while I slept.

It took a solid 30 minutes to calm down and a reassuring promise from the sheriff that he'd come by within the hour to placate me. I checked *every* lock in the house and found none to be out of place.

It's possible that this was an ex who took the photo and passed it to someone else, right?

Maybe some weird kind of revenge for breaking up with them unceremoniously? I had not always been the best partner, sometimes emotionally distant… ok, always emotionally distant. But that's no excuse for this behaviour.

All I had now was time. My parents weren't picking up and bringing this to my friends with my trust levels through the floor made no sense.

So… I hit play and carried on.

I wish I hadn't.

I really, really wish I hadn't.


## Dark Waters


The sounds of water rushing and someone gagging for air fill the speakers as a strange, dark and moody underwater theme plays, one that I don't recognise but whose dissonance and odd sounds put me on edge.

In the blackness, for just a moment, I swear I see a smile barely visible in the murky depths.

My photo is almost unrecognisable now. A mess of black hair covering my pale white scalp, chunks of flesh torn from the face and teeth that should never be seen from behind the cheeks now flashing through.

I look like a monster.

A white title comes up onto the screen and the pit in my stomach expands.

"The 2000 incident."

"Not many people know about this, but Ari was once the subject of a *lot* of attention. They starred in a commercial as a child and garnered national adoration for their role. They were jubilant, cute, and a total natural in front of the camera. For all the positives, however, came negatives. Some fans would fixate on Ari to the point of obsession. This would eventually lead to boundaries being crossed."

A photo of my old family home appears. It's blurry, and the house is dark. It must be the middle of the night. A window on the second floor is open.

My window.

Another photo fades in, this time closer. They're on the property and are using a ladder to climb up, a photo of the uphill journey ahead of them.

A third photo of my bedroom, the flash going off and inevitably spooking me in my sleep.

Stop.

The last photo is of what's behind them as they run, the faint outline of my father chasing them at a distance.

"Ultimately, experts believe that if the family had listened to the letters, heeded the warnings, this would not have occurred, and the rest of the events would not have played out how they did. Sadly, this would send Ari's life on a journey towards one inevitable path… One that I have no doubt is slowly beginning to dawn on them."

Tears stream down my face and I grip my stuffed animal tightly, rocking back and forth in my chair and begging the sheriff to come quicker, but unable to stop myself from watching. I *NEED* to know what the point of this is.

Why would someone do this?

"Ari's original name was Alexandria but was changed to Ari to reflect their gender identity and yet another desire to escape that old life. The sad truth is, they were never ever able to do so." The voice sighed, weariness heavy in their tone. "It makes you wonder how much easier this could've gone, had they just not put up a fight in the first place."

A fade to black and that faint smile visible once again. Nowhere near enough to make out features, save for a smile that made me feel like I was sitting in a shark tank. Emotionless,

hungry and determined.

It was a smile that knew it had its prey where it wanted it.

## The Abyss

On this final segment, the screen remained black as a low drone punctured the air and the narrator spoke.

"You've realised by now that this is a comprehensive video on Ari Monovovich and an admittance of sorts that I myself take a *special* interest in them. But I think it's only fair that I provide this as some evidence for those who find it to follow after the inevitable happens.

Because there's always a beauty in hoping for a happy ending, even if it doesn't come."

I keep telling myself the Sheriff will be here in a few minutes, that everything is locked, and all spaces have been checked, but I don't feel safe. I run my hands across my scar, and I don't. Feel. safe.

"There's a degree of truth that obsessive types can't leave well enough alone, I'm proving that here. But I'm a patient type of obsessive. Because I'm one with a goal to have Ari as mine for all eternity. I came so close before. But… well, it wasn't right. I left a mark to remember me by and sent them on home, never able to truly forget about me, even if they changed every facet of their being."

A video clip of a fish fades onto the screen. It's a deep-sea angler fish, the huge white eyes scanning the depths of the ocean for a sign of prey, the jaws permanently fixed open and large jutting teeth wait to snatch something. It blindly swims around in the inky blackness as the narrator continues, sweat pouring down my head.

"One thing about me for this video, I love the angler fish. A truly remarkable creature that utilises the lure to ensnare its prey. It doesn't need to do anything because it knows that it just needs to send out the right signals and the prey will come to it. Just as you've finally come back to me."

The camera zooms in on the angler fish as the bioluminescent lure begins to move and glow, a beautiful hue that permeates the darkness surrounding it. A small fish spots it and begins swimming closer, the angler fish sits patiently. I feel my knees begin to buckle.

"You did as I knew you would. You saw a channel with your name, Alexandria_Eternal, a theory with your name, and you came right away. They will try to find you and there will be stories, books, and documentaries about where you went. But none of it will ever amount to anything. You will fade into the abyss."

The Angler Fish clamps its jaws down on the fish and, within moments, it is devoured in its entirety.

With that, the video ends.

There's a knock at the door as The Sheriff asks to be let in, the noise sending shivers down my spine and putting me on edge even more-so… He KNOWS I prefer it when people ring the doorbell… I'm glad to have someone taking this seriously, but still…

Does anyone know what I should do?

# FOLIE A DEUX/THE MADNESS OF TWO

"Damn… that storm's getting rough. Hey, what does the 'J' in your name stand for, T.J.?"

I looked up from my position on the foot of the bed, lowering the book in my hands to stare at my twin brother, lounging back in his lazy boy chair.

"Mom never told you? Seems like the sort of thing she'd have had a story ready for."

He shook his head, toes wiggling as he did so. "Nah, she never talked about that stuff with me, always just said you'd know. Thought for the longest time it was an inside joke…" He sighed, pushing the button on his chair to push himself forward. "And it just came to me, so, thought I'd ask."

Mark was a mirror image of me physically—save for my tattoos and his piercings—but emotionally we were vastly different. The misconception so many have about twins is that we think alike, act alike, and even finish each other's sentences. But that's rarely ever true. Just because there's an imprint on our DNA that allows us to look the same doesn't make us the same people. Our Mom figured that out around the third year of parenting, when I would happily sit still for photographs of us dressed identically while Mark stripped naked and peed on the dog. He was the extrovert who loved to sing, to paint beautiful landscapes and breaking artistic men's hearts by the dozens. I was the introvert who enjoyed a good book, writing and had the same steady girlfriend since I was 18.

Still, we were best friends. How could we not be? He shared a womb with me and was my constant companion, as I was his until we discovered there were other people to play board games and go exploring with. Even then, we never faced losing each other to new groups or outside interests. We were secure in that manner. I guess that's the reason we still lived together in our mid-20s. Mark wasn't great at holding down a job, but I loved him all the same. He brought an energy into the home that felt all too comforting.

"Mm, if she didn't tell you, I'm not gonna." I shrugged, smirking as his brow furrowed in playful frustration. The wind outside whipped against the windows and provided a far too dramatic backdrop. He pointed a finger at me, bellowing in his best Shakespearean voice,

"You should never withhold secrets from your womb-mate!" He leaned forward, falling face first onto the floor as he did so, to my amusement.

No sooner had he done so, a thunderclap rang out and during the brief blue flash, I could see a group of tall figures at various distances from the window, all of them staring intently at us. I leapt off the bed and shouted, Mark springing up as I did so.

"Jesus! What the hell was that?" I took a step forward as Mark came to my side, putting a hand on my chest and staring at the window.

"I wouldn't, man. Let me go look, okay?" He flashed a grin in my direction before taking a shaky step forward. "Can't have you hogging the glory if you've seen an alien!"

A few tense moments pass and as he reaches the window of our living room, he stares, shoulders heaving.

"Well…?" I press, still clutching my book in my hand.

He turns back to me, sweat dripping from his forehead and his jet-black hair matted as identical green eyes meet my own.

"Don't answer the door. Please." He mutters, the rhythmic knock of the front door perfectly on cue.

I shudder, seeing my brother, the life of any party and a man who takes the notion of danger as seriously as a clown may take a funeral THIS terrified was unnerving. He was my safety blanket, and I found myself unwilling to answer the door, but unable to resist asking, "Who's there?" As Mark's eyes widened in horror and shook his head vigorously at me.

From the other side of our front door, a soft scratching dragged itself from the bottom of the door frame to the tips of the corners before a more aggressive, singular thump rang out.

"I'm… I'm begging you…" the small voice called. It was soft and filled with pain. "You will die in there if you don't… so please… for me… for us…" it scratched again, frantically.

"I… I don't know who you ar—" I began, Mark pulling his hand over my face and away from the door before I could finish.

"You didn't see what I saw, but they are NOT here to help us, T.J." He whispered, his heart beating so hard it was punching me in the back. "Stay. Away."

We stood there in silence for a moment before a whimpering echoed from the door, followed by the same soft voice growing louder with every syllable.

"Doesn't know who I… he says he… why doesn't he… why don't you… how dare you…"

The thumping now threatened to pull the door off its hinges as the figure on the other side bellowed, a voice far removed from the pleading one just a moment ago.

"HOW COULD YOU FORGET ME? WE WILL FIND A WAY IN. WE WILL. WE WILL. WE WILL." With every affirmation, another smash on the door, another clap of lightning and a horrifying glimpse at the figures outside, now coming closer.

Mark stepped away from me to shut the curtains and ushered me to my bedroom, darting into the kitchen to get some essentials before shouting "ONE SEC, WE'LL NEED THIS!", the sound of rummaging and his nervous but jaunty singing of the Doom song ringing out amid the thumping of the door and wind outside as he reappeared with our dads old shotgun, barricading the door and planting himself on the beanbag by my bed, loading the gun with haste as I stood there, dumbfounded.

"Mark, what the hell is going on? What is with that storm outside?" I pressed him, clearly, he knew something I didn't, and the rush of adrenaline was letting emotions I'd normally suppress come up. Mark's shameful gaze away from my eyes and back to the door only emboldened me further.

"It's better if you don't know for the time being, T.J. You're not ready and I'm not willing to let you go to… to them out there…" he loaded the last shell and cocked the gun with authority. "YA HEAR THAT? THE GUNS LOADED."

"Mark, answer the fucking question. NOW." I stood up, being kept out of the loop in an already confusing situation like this was too much to take. I stormed over to him and put my hand on the barrel of the gun, pointing it away from us. "Put that stupid fucking thing down and TALK to me. We've just gone from zero to a hundred in a manner of MINUTES, and you won't say why. You know everything about me. Why isn't it the same way with you? I don't know about your boyfriends until you break up with them, I don't see your art until it's finished, or even hear about any of your issues until they're resolved… what the hell is it with you?!" I lower my voice as my lip trembles, genuine pain slipping through. "Why won't you share with me?"

Mark's eyes flash and while avoiding contact he mutters, "I'm the older twin, gotta protect you. You're Mom's favourite, you'd never understand…"

The sensation that went through my chest in that moment was a mixture of fear and anger. To think he'd shut me out to this degree…

"Will you take your hands off of the g—"

*BOOM*

The shot rang out, and it knocked both of us back. I slipped and knocked my bedside cabinet over. Pills, notes, and a bedside photograph smashing on the floor as I hit the ground with a thud. Once my eyes adjusted and the ringing in my ears faded, I looked over to see if it hurt Mark, but he was thankfully just a little twitchy, now pointing back at the door with shaky hands as I checked myself for scrapes. None, thank god.

"You're a fucking idiot, Mark." I breathed, steadying myself as he looked over.

"Wouldn't be the fun twin if I wasn't, T.J." A slight smile flickering across his face as we both let out nervous laughter.

I picked up the contents on the floor and pulled the photo out of the now broken frame, a photo of me and Mark pulling our best wrestler poses in suits at our mom's wedding to our stepdad a year ago. I spotted some writing on the corner of the photo, not obscured by the frame, but before I could read it, a new sound greeted us that chilled me to my core.

A howl that began at an ear piercingly high pitch, forcing me to cover my ears. I looked to Mark, but he didn't flinch, instead keeping his sights trained on the door and shouting something I couldn't make out over the deafening sound, the pitch lowering as it got closer to the door.

The lights flickered, the wind raged, and everything felt like it was teetering on an edge. Helplessness was the overarching sensation as my world darkened.

"WHAT DO YOU WANT?" I cried out, apropos of nothing, hoping in vain I'd get some kind of reply.

In an instant, everything fell silent, the howling quietened, and I could hear a shuffling sound behind the bedroom door as it tried the handle before a soft, older voice than before replied:

"We want you to come with us. Where you belong. Where it's safe."

From the window, we heard the sentiment "where you belong" echoed, amplified in the eerie silence, absent of violence or weather interference.

"Safe? What do you mean? You guys have been trying to—"

"You can't go with them, T.J." Mark had stood up, his gun pointing at me and eyes wide, tears streaming down his face and catching in his neat beard. "You would never be safe with them. You'd always be incomplete, always in doubt. I'm the elder twin, I have to protect you." His hands were shaking, but his aim was true. I could tell he meant what he said, and his intent was in the air. Not malicious, but determined.

"Mark, what have you done?"

"It's not what I've done… it's what THEY'VE done!" He nodded to the window and the door. "THEY have pushed it to this point, to us being here. I knew they were coming, and I was ready. I'm always prepared. They want you to go through so much pain, so much suffering, and even THEY don't know if you'll survive. I can't let them do that to you, T.J." He began crying. "I can't watch my better self-go through such anguish, not without me."

My head throbbed. A migraine from the thunderstorm, maybe? No, it was more rapid than that, like I'd done this before… but where?

Lowering my hands slowly, I sat down on the bed as Mark breathed heavily, keeping the gun trained on me. I looked around the room and tried to keep myself calm. My eyes fell on the photo of us, the writing in the corner… and then I understood.

"Mark, you asked me what the J meant in my name, that Mom never told you?" I looked at him. He nodded quickly.

"One of the few things she kept from me, yeah. I'd meant to ask you before, but something always came up…" He sniffed, wiping his face with his sleeve. He was calming down. That was good.

"Well, I guess it's understandable you wouldn't know, I didn't always have it growing up. We used to share everything, didn't we? I remember when we binged *Dragonball Z* as kids, we spent summer nights building Saiyan pods out of blankets and communicating through walkie talkies. I was always Vegeta, and you were always Nappa, the strong but eccentric one."

Mark smiled. The howling began creeping softly back up the longer he held the gun at me. "Or how we would ask Mom to cut the crusts off of my sandwich, leave the other for you and then switch them last minute to mess with her. We used to drive her crazy pulling twin magic on her. You'd always cover for me if I got grounded and it'd always result in her grounding us both. You never minded being with me throughout it all and you never complained, not once."

"I remember when you came out to me, we were 17, and you were acting weird around me because Aaron Jensen had said I was his best friend, and I couldn't understand why you were so upset. But then you asked me how I felt when I looked at Macy and I got it straight away. We sat up all night figuring out how you could get Aaron's attention the next day and sure enough…"

"I drew him unflatteringly and said I'd do it better if he came over for a nude portrait." We laughed, tears sliding down Mark's upturned lips as we punctuated this room of fear with a moment of pure joy. We could hear the scratching on the door becoming more panicked as the howling rose in pitch, but we kept talking.

"You remember when Dad died? We stood by his side and held his hand as he went. He looked at me and said I would be the storyteller his family had dreamt of… and when he looked at you, what did he say?"

"He said I would carry the good, bad and ugly of our family legacy with me in my art… and he sure as hell wasn't wrong."

"No, he wasn't… Dad was more perceptive than I think either of us realised as teens." I got to my feet, staring at the photo, gripping it far too tightly as the voice from behind the door cooed at me.

"That's it… you're doing so well… you'll be with us soon.…" I couldn't tell if it was malicious or just elated, but the scratching and knocking was becoming too fast to seem sane or even human. Mark took a step forward as I got up and his voice grew panicked.

"T.J.… I will not let you go to them. I don't want to do this, I'm begging you… please, sit down and I will handle this. I promise. Just…" He cocked the gun again, but I carried on staring.

"The J wasn't always there. I added it later in life, something happened, and I had to commemorate that moment the only way I knew how." I turned and stared my twin in the face, that eager spirit long gone, the light and zest he had replaced by paranoia and psychosis. My mirror image is an emaciated mess.

Tears now running down my face, I started reading as he screamed at me to stop, the lights flickering furiously.

*Boys,*

*You are the light of my world and having you here on my wedding day to your stepfather was the greatest blessing I could have received. I know your father would be happy for me, and I see so much of him in both of you every single day.*
*Theo, Jacob, I love you both more than you could ever know.*
*You don't know it yet, but you've made a mark on this world that nobody will ever forget.*

*—Mom*

I took another step forward.

"The weather was horrific, you'd moved out a month earlier and said you needed your own space. You wouldn't tell me why or what had happened. Your messages got more sparse as time went on and I hadn't seen you in a week, so I drove over after work."

His face sagged, grimacing into a vile caricature of rage as he shook. The lights grew so bright before flickering again.

"You didn't answer your phone and there was one light on in your flat. Your front door was locked, and my spare key wasn't working. I could hear your favourite song in the background, and I knew something was wrong. I tried knocking, but you said…"

"I didn't know who you were. Like I don't right now, no brother who loves me would want to go with *them*," he snarled, spit flying from his slack jaw, teeth melting and falling onto the floor with clumps of his skin. I took another step forward. It pushed the barrel against my chest. But I had to do this. The howling was so loud I thought my eardrums would burst.

"I broke the door down and you locked yourself in the bedroom with dad's shotgun. I begged for you to come out but… but…" My stomach contracted and I felt the bile rise, but I had to do this. His face stripped of flesh, muscle and bone exposed to the lights, brain matter splattering over the floor and dripping down his cheeks. His one good eye looking at me, bloodshot.

He couldn't speak anymore, just whimpered. I took one last step forward and held him in my arms.

"I took your name because I couldn't handle the idea of you being away from me. I called you Mark because what it left in those memories was a wound that I couldn't deal with. But look where that got me…"

I let him go, my visage of him returning to the normal, happy brother I remembered for a moment, the shotgun in my hands and the police sirens outside wailing as my mom cried against the bedroom door, begging for my life so she wouldn't have to bury her other son.

I looked up at him, the version of him I wanted to remember, but knew what it would do to me if I did. The hedonistic, outgoing, considerate elder twin that had tried for so long to keep his demons at bay, before succumbing to them. The ugly legacy of our family proved too much for him in his fight and inevitably manifesting in me.

He smiled at me, the way I remembered him doing so. My smile. The one I hadn't seen either of us in so, so long. I put the gun down and walked towards the door.

"You've got a long road ahead of you if you go with them. I won't be there to help you… you know that, right? I don't have all the answers." He called after me, the light hitting his face just right and making him look radiant, the way I idolised him in my mind.

I pulled on the handle, nodding.

"I know, but look on the bright side… now you know what the J stands for."

# HAVE YOU LOST YOUR SHADOW?

It must sound so silly, losing track of something that's attached to you. I'm sure some folks already have a *The sun went down, didn't it?* statement at the ready.

But I'm being serious. I haven't seen my shadow since the beginning of the summer solstice.

It's remarkable how easily we come to accept mundane oddities as just a part of our everyday lives, brushing the only piece of our skeleton that sits outside of our flesh twice a day, experiencing moments of no breathing followed by choking during heavy sleep… and our shadow. That long, featureless, black frame that looms over all that we do. A silent participant that we only occasionally pay any attention to on particularly slow days or where our shadow sits in a largely unique spot.

I suppose I'm trying to make it more glamorous than it actually is. I guess I have an admiration for the odd things we accept as normalcy.

My full body shadow was no different to anyone else's, a simple tall, thin figure that walked and moved in sync with me. I did, however, have a skill manipulating parts of it:

Shadow puppetry. I revelled in making fun and fantastical creatures by bending my fingers in just the right way. My friends loved it, my family even more so. Dogs, cats, dragons, and alpacas, I found such joy in bringing them to life or testing myself to find new ways to captivate audiences. I was a born entertainer and an artist.

But on occasion, I'd feel the urge to snap my digits in unusual ways. Never painful, or at least it never *felt* painful, but it sure as hell looked it to anyone privy to the "show", I'm sure. My pinkie would tuck itself underneath my ring finger, wrapping itself around as the joints stretched and strained, other fingers accommodating while my wrists jerked and shuddered.

On the screen was a different story, fantastical shadow cities filled with great spires, Georgian manor houses, market stalls filled with hungry, vibrant souls. My hands could make more than anyone imagined. Eventually, the shows grew from the backyards and school talent shows to being booked in Sturgeon's grand hall, opening for The Fabulous DeKoltas, a troupe of gymnasts, vantablack manipulators and nightmare catchers.

My act would involve using my fingers and toes, a bright spotlight, and a LOT of improvisation. People would flock to anywhere my name was on the marquee in hopes of visiting "The Umbra Citadel", seeing the ongoings of the town and its strange inhabitants.

In time, the shadows would take on their own life, though I'd never tell my audiences such a thing. Characters would wander off to the edges of the screen and test the boundaries. Audiences thought it was peak surrealism and heaped praise on me. One character people gravitated towards was "The Conjurer", a reclusive man hidden behind a thick coat and a layered pointy hat, occasionally seen casting shadows with his own hands.

"How the hell do you do that? Shadows within shadows? This is avant-garde shadow puppetry! Such a thing… it's inconceivable!" My manager commented after a show a few months ago, enthralled and frightened by my abilities. What he *thought* were my abilities.

"Ah… can't reveal my secrets now, can I?" I chuckled, stretching my hands and feet, joints aching terribly now the adrenaline wore off. Arthritis was almost certainly in my future.

"You're killin' me, Will! Come on, you've made it this far. The Nexus wants to interview you and hear about how it's all done ahead of your television debut!" I could practically see the dollar signs in his eyes, but I knew his heart was in the right place… even if that happened to be next to his wallet.

"Alright, Jennings, alright. Tell their best journalist I'll fill them in when the date is set, okay? A tell-all interview."

He grinned and practically jumped out of his shoes at the prospect, clapping and thanking me as he left, someone else manoeuvring past him to get through the doorway to my dresser. A tall, thin man in a beautiful red suit, bright silver blazer and bright smile, his satchel affixed to his side perfectly, a small bump pushing its way up from the inside as if something was writhing deep within its bowels.

Eustace DeKolta.

"I know your secret, Mr. Meijer." He offered out a gloved hand. I took it and we shook firmly, keeping my eyes on his, though they were obscured behind dark circular glasses. "Your shadow has a mind of its own."

"Well… Jung says the Shadow is an Id, perhaps mine is simply the unconscious desires I have wanting to break free, eh?" I smirked, grabbing a drink, and swirling it in my hand. "Come on, really?"

DeKolta's smile faded, and his shoulders shook as if a cold shiver came over him.

"Being cynical of the things you don't understand will not do you any favours. It will only bring ruin as it did for me. A shadow person may be attached to you, but it is like any living creature… push it far enough, poke and prod it unprovoked… it will bite back." He cocked his head to the side, looked at something behind me and the smirk returned. "You fear it, don't you? This is why the lights are fixed the way they are, to trap it… to stop it gaining too much power."

I felt uncomfortable. How was he this astute with just a handful of interactions with me?

"Look, I don't know about any kind of shadow person or whatever. But… I will admit that my shows have gotten out of hand, no pun intended. There're things going on in it that I'm not in full control of. Sometimes it feels like it's getting away from me. I know there's places in The Umbra Citadel that I haven't shown the crowd yet, that I don't *want* to show." I shook my head, downing my stiff drink. "But that's just fatigue talking. I've been at this for 20 fucking years. I'm in control."

I stood up and gestured for him to leave. He shook his head and smirked, turning on his heel as he headed for the door.

"When you feel the chains binding him begin to crack, seek me. If they break, do not run another show. Good luck, Will." He bowed and exited, leaving me with a mixture of exhaustion and concern.

As I turned my back to sit down, the light from the hallway caught my eye and I saw my shadow.

Nestled up against the wall, watching me.

*******

As the summer solstice kicked in, it became harder and harder to find locations where either my skills weren't sought after, or shadows didn't permeate every aspect of Sturgeon's structures. Even at night, mandatory media obligations filled with brightly lit locations meant I was not only dragging my shadow along with me, but subjecting parts of it to the torment of Shadow Puppetry. Twisting and pulling it until the core essence revealed itself and The Umbra Citadel would form.

I'd figured out by this point that not only was I not in control of the complex shadow puppetry, but I was being inexorably pulled towards The Conjurer and their journey to the great gates deep within the bowels of The Umbra Citadel. My feet burned and veins popped as the last handful of shows I performed began to showcase the more forbidden areas of the city, rituals the black sea-faring sailors would undertake, the harvest under a black star, the day-care where everyone sleeps upside down.

I hated it. I hated every moment of it. But the crowd became more rabid with every show, growing aggressive if I wasn't on stage for longer than an hour. It began to get ugly. I would rarely see the crowd from the bright lights and focusing on my art, but I'd hear mumblings from other acts that the crowd were pallid, unrecognisable and feral.

Then, one night after a particularly rowdy show... I got sloppy.

Maybe it was exhaustion. Maybe it was an unconscious desire to have things just calm down for a while. But in the lead-up to my "tell-all interview", I stayed up late far too many times to perfect a new technique, falling asleep in front of my spotlight on the fifth night.

When I woke up, there was no shadow. Not when my hands poked out, my feet or my whole body. An absence of space where my companion once stood.

Fuck.

I darted for the door, grabbing my phone and my keys, checking my messages, and finding Eustace's number.

Instead, I found a post on The Nexus about a "new art show by Shadow Artist William Meijer TONIGHT ONLY!"

Oh.

Oh no.

Eustace's words came back, and the realisation hit me with a wave of fear: If my shadow isn't here, where the fuck is it?

I felt that concern as I ran for the grand hall, the sun setting, and the shadows cast by every building, animal, car, and object seemed to be reaching out to me. Whether to stop me or help me, I don't know.

By the time I got to the hall, it was a sold-out show. The damn ticket officer wouldn't even acknowledge me. Back turned and staring at the floor, swaying from side to side in a rhythmic fashion, fixated on something unseen. I didn't have time to argue, I pushed past and ran through the back area to find Eustace.

The sounds I heard as I passed by the general seating area were horrific, animalistic, and manic. The sounds of things being torn, gurgling with a soft, almost pleading moan snuffed out with a dull thud, closed mouth shrieks increasing in volume and agony as something wet is pulled free. Whooping, hollering and incomprehensible noises that I tried my absolute best to block out, but left me shaking to my very core and grateful I didn't see them. I never wanted to find out what matched those fucking noises.

Finding the DeKolta dresser, I found Eustace unconscious on the floor, satchel gone and head bleeding.

"Eustace… Eustace! I can't do this without you man, come on!" I turned him over and gave him some gentle slaps. Thankfully, rousing him from unconsciousness. A grim look on his face.

"You did a show, you let it loose. The Conjurer you spoke of opened up the gates."

I felt a lump in my throat. The noises outside weighing down on me with every passing second.

"What do I do?" I asked, knees buckling with nerves. "I want to make this right, to fix this."

Eustace shook his head, getting to his feet.

"Your shadow was called back to the Umbra Citadel. It has left you forever. Vulnerable."

He walked to the door and set off for the hallway. I followed behind him, still determined to fix my error.

"Vulnerable? Why? Eustace, please tell me we can fix this!" I pulled on his shoulder, but he brushed me off, walking silently down the hall until we got to the stage door.

"You're vulnerable because without a shadow, your soul is up for grabs. No barrier, no protector. Anything sees you as fair game now." He shook his head and turned round, taking off the glasses and showcasing a scar running the length of one eye, a grey pupil staring back at me. "You can't fix everything. You have to own your mistakes. Get a new shadow, Will. Ask for one or steal one if you have to. But your journey stops here."

He opened the door, and we stepped out onto the stage, the screen no longer running and not a soul in the audience. The smell of iron mixed with a miasma of foul odours hitting my nostrils and bringing me to my knees.

As my perspective shifted, I saw what lay in every seat of the audience area.

Shadows. An entire hall full of them silently sat there, watching.

Eustace flipped a light switch, and they were gone in an instant. He mentioned something about trying to reclaim the lost people eventually, but that it would take time. Said he had a tournament to appear in first.

As for me, I kept a low profile and refused any and all interviews. Told them I was sick and mentally exhausted, unwilling to answer any scrutinising questions or condemnations of what happened to these people.

To my horror, that was not why most were inquiring. Instead, they were eager, almost too eager for another show. Demanding, I ran it again and opened the doors to the Umbra Citadel, stating that every night their shadows stood over them and demanded it silently.

Some, however, asked in an almost mocking tone, "Where is your shadow now? Do you feel safe?"

I hear odd noises outside during the waning hours. Things call to me, in an almost singing tone, to come outside. They don't say it, but I know that's what they mean. Every food delivery I get is handled with minimal physical contact. I tell the driver to leave the food on the doorstep and I snatch it when they're gone.

Last week, I caught him watching me from the bushes. He stood up slowly as he spotted me, his shoulders hunching over and something pushing up through his uniform. I slammed the door before I saw anymore and switched food companies. Maybe they're not everywhere.

I've given up on sleeping for long, now I just dream of the Umbra Citadel. In shadow, I walk along the cobbled streets and to the lair of The Conjurer. He asks me questions without speaking, talks about the lost shadows, he pleads for me to come home.

I need to get back. I need to go there.

I need to be able to sleep at night.

I'm begging someone, anyone, to tell me they too lost track of their shadow.

Or, better yet, someone who found their shadow again.

And, if you did…

Can I have it?

# THERE'S ONLY EMBERS AT THE END

"Would you mind telling me what happened?"

"Are you sure? It's a little on the long-winded side. I know how you hate things that go on and on…"

"Well, the way I see it, we have all the time in the world. Given the unique place we're in."

"The unique place? Where are you referring to?"

He smiled.

"Everywhere."

## I

Never underestimate the lengths someone will go to so they can fulfil a lifelong desire.

As I sat in my room with my list of essential items, as dictated by the book, I contemplated how I'd even gotten here some months prior. It's astounding how just one piece of information, one decision, one solitary but powerful emotion can push a person to places they never thought they'd go to.

But here I am, wrapping up the head of a deer in delicate parchment paper, careful to ensure that it's folded 47 times. Not 48, not 50, 47. The blood soaking through the bottom and giving it a crimson hue that paired well with the beige. Beside it sat a serrated hunting knife, the bone of an elk, the skull of an owl, 2 incisors from a bear and a small mixing bowl with various herbs.

All given without resistance or pain, as the book dictated.

I carefully placed them into a burlap sack, tightened it and placed that in my hiker's backpack before donning my winter gear and getting my dog, Bastion, before heading out the door.

I knew I may not ever come back again.

The Doorway, said to be guarded by the mythical lord Janus, has been referenced in many cultures and across the millennia by scholars. What lay beyond it, of course, differs from person to person. Treasures, curses, god itself, you can take your pick. Some say the door manifests to wandering travellers when they least expect it, offering them whatever their heart desires at the cost of something unseen, likely their sanity or an empirical value, they would have no way of knowing about at the present moment in time like an unborn son. Others postulate that it appears to only those chosen by the gods, with the right blood and belief systems in place.

But the most scintillating of practices and rumours are the ones found in The Book of Gnomes that, after a decade of tireless searching, had finally come into my possession. They gave the most likely of answers to the location of the door. One stooped in ancient human culture: Offerings.

Written roughly in the 8th century and translated largely in secret during the dark ages, it contains the secrets of England's woods and the ancient creatures that dwell within it. To my benefit, an entire section was focused on anomalous entities and locations, like The Doorway.

Before we go any further, I feel I should be forthright with my reasoning for spending 10 years of my life looking for ways to access this possibly fictitious door in human folklore. I feel I owe you that explanation before taking any more of your time. Though, for the sake of what is going to unfold, I am going to keep it simple and ask that you trust me.

I believe there is something beyond the doorway that houses a treasure greater than any riches, something that would change my life irrevocably.

And I am determined to find it.

I travelled some 100 miles south until I got to what we call The New Forest. The name belies the ancient nature of the land. It's been there for well over 12,000 years. Even as recently as the Iron Age some two millennia ago, these forests were there, watching and proliferating as man grew and expanded, becoming the resting place of royalty who died in battle. Now, if you were to visit, it's regarded as a national treasure. Great swathes of trees tower against the sky, the deeper in you go, blotting out much of the sun's rays, hiding its greater secrets.

The darker places of the forest were where I had to traverse. My golden retriever Bastion bounding on ahead, eager to be in such a large space and likely excited to run after any Donkeys, Horses, Cows or even Deer that he might spot.

"Your paces must exceed 700 as you travel into the heart of the New Forest, following its great veins to the hidden source. Eventually, you will come upon a rock face that has been untouched for untold millennia with a moss growing across its left side. Upon the light of a new moon… This is where your offering must begin."

Beneath, a small phrase etched in a scratchy black font that stood apart from the rest:

**All is well, but a blackened seed has taken root, we must unearth it.**

Sure enough, my Fitbit indicated I was at 836 paces and following a large trunk barely hidden by the underbrush when the great rock face came into view. Greyed and towering, the moss only growing on the left side like a birthmark, I knew I'd found what I was looking for.

I put a bookmark on the page, setting down my bag and knowing I had another hour until the sun would fully set, I decided to check the area with Bastion before sitting down and preparing myself for what was to come.

They say you can't exorcise your demons, but you can sure as hell learn to make peace with them.

## II

The first time I caught sight of "The Other" was when I was a child of about 5, sat playing in front of the mirror and chatting away to my reflection. I suppose in a child's mind, those kinds of irregularities are met less with immediate horror and instead with curiosity.

As I looked closely, I noticed my reflection tilting its head ever so slightly more than I was, the eyes widening in understanding as it perceived me while I perceived it. I stopped blinking, taking in more of its features as the skin tightened and stretched across the jawline, causing deep crevasses in the sides as it became gaunt. The hair once matching my own brown curls, fraying, and thinning out as the skull expanded.

My mirror was set in a way so that the door to my playroom could be seen and as my heart began to beat faster, the door opened and a figure stood in the archway, blinded by the light.

I had no perception of who it was, my mind simply went to "parent", and I watched as it pointed to my reflection, to the "other me", whose head was still tilting down at a horrifying angle, practically snapping under the weight of its insistence to keep turning.

Then, without any warning, it smacked against the glass, a horrible cracking sound that I can still hear to this day.

That action finally broke my stare, and the haze faded away as I screamed, turning to my door and expecting my Mum or Dad to ask what was wrong.

But the door was still shut.

Mum came in soon after, soothing me as I talked about "The bad man" in the mirror and assured me it was just a dream.

But from that day forward, on certain occasions, I would catch glimpses of The Other changing in the mirror. Always watching, always wanting out.

And the doorway behind him permanently opened.

## III

The sun had set, and I unzipped my backpack, unfurled the burlap sack, and took out the book again, Bastion sleeping by my side and still gently gnawing on his favourite stuffed animal.

"Once you are in front of the rock face, you must apply the powers of man, starting with that which provides us all life." Next to it, the image of a door and another inscription:

**There is something amiss, but you can't quite place it. Something is burning.**

I took out the hunting knife and sliced my palm, letting the blood flow freely as I drew the outline of a door as instructed and bandaged my hand up when the job was done.

"Next, the strength of the wanderer with which to provide balance and sustainability. How much have these bones seen?"

I affixed the Elk bones at the side, acting as the hinges.

"Then, the wisdom and foresight of the Owl. A great predator who sees all. What did they see when they gazed upon you? Will they provide you a handle with which to grasp your truth? Your destiny?"

The owl skull. I placed it to the right, acting as a door handle. My access.

"Your offering must be left in the centre. The beast behind the door must be placated, for while it is blind, it is not dumb. Show it respect and do not gaze upon its entry. Turn your back and wait until the light of the full moon shines on you. This will be your sign to proceed."

I unwrapped the deer's head and did as instructed, leaving it in front of my macabre door of bone and blood before taking Bastion and going for a walk. If this didn't work, you could classify me as a psychopath and lock me up for all I cared.

After all, I had no plan forward if this failed.

## IV

There are many moments in even the most mundane person's life that they can point to as the best, the worst, and life changing. I certainly have a few that stick out.

The difference is… all of mine are linked to The Other.

The first time I made the connection was at the age of 7. The playroom mirror long since relegated to the attic and a built-in wardrobe mirror in its place. Not that it mattered.

In the middle of the night on a hot summer's eve, I awoke to the sound of soft tapping against glass. Even with these occasional bizarre experiences, I was terrified by the notion of someone tangible outside my bedroom window, some stranger danger situation.

*Tap, tap, tap.*

It took me a few minutes to finally open my bedroom curtains, only to show nothing there. Before I could breathe a sigh of relief, I caught sight of my mirror in the moonlight reflection.

The Other was sitting there, cross-legged and tapping away with a bony, dirty fingernail.

I don't know why I always succumbed to its whims in the first instance. Maybe there was something mesmerising about the way it lured me in. Maybe these things have the innate ability to suppress our fears long enough to strike. But all I know is I obeyed the tap and walked over, sitting down in my Buzz Lightyear pyjamas, and observing The Other me. His were of Woody, tattered and frayed in places, large bags under his eyes and sallow skin, but a far more humane appearance about him. Perhaps he wasn't trying to scare me?

He took his nail away and simply observed me, yellowed eyes taking in every inch of me and frowning as he saw my pyjamas did not match his own. But no sooner had he expressed his disappointment than he switched to something akin to joy, smiling with rotten teeth as he pointed to the bedroom door.

That sinking feeling you get when you miss a step on the stairs immediately hit me as my Nana walked through the doorway, great light still rippling through it. She stumbled in an awkward manner, as if she'd hurt her leg.

It was only when she bent down to look at me that I realised why, tears in my eyes and screaming as I backed away from the mirror like a cornered animal and ran to my parents' bedroom.

Nana's eyes were rolled into the back of her head. The left half of her once jovial face dropped as if pulled down by tenterhooks, tongue lolling out of her mouth and blood pouring from her eyes, nose, and ears.

She was having a stroke.

The very next day, we got the call.

Nana had died from a burst aneurysm in her brain on the way to the bathroom in the middle of the night, roughly around 4am. Instantaneous and without suffering.

In layman's terms, she'd died from a stroke.

I avoided my mirror for years after that.

## V

Bastion nudged me out of my meditation, his soft nose getting under my arm and demanding head pets. Can't say I blame him, he's downright adorable.

I don't think I'd have made this journey without him by my side.

We sat there for a little while, enjoying the calm serenity of nature and the enjoyment of each other's company as my mind idly wandered while he wagged his tail, grateful to get his best friend's full attention.

But the quiet serenity of the woods was not to last, broken by three things in quick succession,

The low hum of something stirring underneath the ground. Something large.

The birds, insects, reptiles, and mammals all scattering from our area, as if knowing something was coming.

The sounds of a great oaken door being opened after a long absence, hinges creaking under the strain and the low hum turning into a drone, not dissimilar to the growl of a great beast that stalked the lands long ago.

From my position, sitting behind a log and facing away from the doorway I'd created, I saw the ugly light shine out from its archway and bathe the surrounding land in its corruption. I wish I could equate it to something within our colour spectrum, but words fail me. It was alluring and revolting all at once, something I would struggle to put into any arbitrary box we had.

Bastion, to his credit, tried to keep his whimpered noises to a minimum and instead buried his head in my lap, seemingly knowing to keep quiet and stay away from whatever the hell was there.

Every cell in my body screamed to flee, to get away from this imminent threat. A dense fog joined the ugly light and a fetid stench hit my nostrils, making my eyes water and my gag reflex kick in. I wanted to vomit, to scream, but I held my nerve.

I'd spent 10 fucking years waiting for this moment, this occurrence that most would simply laugh off and relegate to the land of the fantastical.

I would not waste it here.

Hands shaking and heart lodged in my throat, I closed my eyes, steeled my resolve as this beast looked around for its offering and tried to tune out the smells and sounds, going back into my mind and reminding myself of how I got here.

Why I took this journey in the first place.

VI

The Other Me would only pop up a handful of times from that day forward, partly because I avoided standing in front of any mirror too long and kept the damn thing covered in my room at all times.

But you cannot stop a force that you do not fully understand.

It lay dormant for so long that as I grew into adulthood, my mature mind simply rationalised away the experiences as that of an overactive imagination from an only child largely isolated from others.

But that was impossible to accept once I turned 19.

My first few months away from home and in my own dorm should've, by all accounts, been the time of my life. I had freedom unrestricted, several great dorm mates, and a course I was passionate about. University is, after all, a time you're supposed to look back on fondly.

For me, that first year was nothing short of hell.

The mirror in my dorm was at the far end of my small room, our dorms were individual bedrooms and each flat housed 7 rooms. They weren't bespoke by today's standards, but 11 years ago, it was seen as well worth the money.

I'd been on a boozy night out as the first week or so of term is collectively known as "Freshers Week", a time to acclimate to your new surroundings, make friends, get laid and generally get the fuck around part of your energy out of your system.

I remember laying there, embracing the drunken high and enjoying the room spinning whilst ensuring I didn't move too much and enact the not-so-fun projectile vomit part of having too much. I knew I'd struggle to make it to my bathroom.

I'd had my eyes closed for maybe 10 minutes when I heard the sound of familiar footsteps. Any anxious child growing up would get used to the various cadences a family member's feet would make. Slow and plodding for mum, thudding and powerful for dad, fast and energetic for the family dog.

So, when I heard the latter traipsing into my room, I was beset with confusion and apprehension. Knowing full well my Golden Barney was 200+ miles away at our family home.

I sat up carefully, looking around and noticing a glimpse of light coming from my mirror, but unable to see much without my glasses. I clumsily reached for them before stumbling over.

I sobered up immediately as I became transfixed by the sight in front of me.

The Other stood there, relishing in its horrifying frame. Standing far taller than I and barely resembling me in form, the dead eyes bulging out of large sockets, black veins visible underneath translucent skin and a cone-like skull stretching upwards with barely any hair.

But it was the fact he was petting my dog that scared me the most.

Barney looked fine. Thankfully, no deformities or damage to him. But the thing that gave me pause was how youthful he looked. Our Barney was 13 years old, barely able to stand up, and couldn't even say goodbye to me when I'd left for university. This one looked to be maybe 4 or 5, just how I remembered him as a child.

The Other Me didn't take his eyes off me as he pet Barney, as if he knew something I didn't. He looked up and down my body and disgust filled his eyes, taking a step towards me. Then he spoke. A voice not dissimilar to mine but steeped in damage and sorrow, like I'd been wailing for a decade and my vocal cords were long since fried.

"You are ungrateful. You are undeserving."

As I took one more look down at Barney, I recoiled in horror. His familiar happy face was an unrecognisable mess, like someone had scrubbed away any features of his that were distinctive to me. Now, he barely looked like a dog. I couldn't even tell what he was supposed to be, save for the form he took. It was horrible.

"I want." It croaked, reaching a malformed hand out towards me. "I take."

The Doorway swung open and two shrouded figures stood in the archway, beckoning to him. He recoiled and reluctantly pulled back, smirking as my own door burst open to the sound of partying from my housemates.

"Come party man, I know you've got more in you!" One of them chimed, blasting music from the living room.

But their smiles faded as the light shone on my face.

"Dude, why are you crying?"

The next morning, my mum called me to tell me that based on Barney's age and difficulties, the vet had put him down in our kitchen and he'd gone peacefully, though I was angry and devastated that I couldn't be there. He was my best friend growing up and I should've been there to say goodbye.

You know what they say, though.

When it rains, it pours.

# VII

The noises by the doorway grew in intensity and ferocity as this thing hungered for sustenance. The closest thing I can equate it to is a bear foraging for food after a long hibernation, primal, fierce, unrelenting.

As it stumbled over my offering, it gave way to some of the most disgusting sounds of consumption I've ever heard. A mukbang directly into my ear canal that I desperately wanted to mute. If you're into that stuff, more power to you. To me, it is simply grotesque to hear anything masticating up against my eardrums.

Soon, the noises faded, and the unseen beast retreated back behind the door, taking the stench, the colour and the fog with it, but the low hum remained.

I opened The Book of Gnomes and continued reading, not content enough with the silence to move just yet.

"If the beast accepts your offering, you may pass through the doorway and find what you seek. But be aware of the pitfalls when traversing an unknown place. This cavernous maw houses many ways to ensnare you, trick you, and keep you within its bowels for an eternity. Take your light with you, hold your memento close and do not stray from the path. All the ins are out."

I took a deep breath and got up from my spot, grabbing my flashlight and the chosen memento, taking the mixed bowl of herbs and pouring them into a small bottle of water and pouring over my arms, legs and face. Something to do with warding off anything nefarious. I did the same with Bastion, though he admittedly tried to eat the mixture. Can't blame him.

The Doorway was gargantuan, built in a way as if it'd always been a part of the rock-face and the sort of thing you'd see featured on a documentary about ancient civilisations and how the hell they could build such a thing: a singular grand oaken door with a handle the size of my head, still made out of the owl's skull but amplified. Various sigils and shapes were carved into the frame, interweaving across the huge span of wood before coalescing and forming a strange central sign in the centre where a peephole sat. If someone was looking through it, I couldn't tell.

I looked at the memento I'd chosen, a broken watch from the 80s I'd strapped around my wrist. It shimmered in the moonlight, and I could faintly see something stirring in the reflection, but I dared not stare too long. Not when I was so close.

Bastion licked my hand, sensing my apprehension. I knelt down and gave his forehead a kiss out of gratitude. He was a good boy.

"Alright buddy, are you ready? You gotta stick close to me. I don't know what we'll find in there." I breathed, he licked his nose and put a paw on my knee, his own way of confirming.

With everything in hand, I left my backpack by the doorway and placed a shuddering hand on the handle before pushing down and opening it, stepping into the darkness.

## VIII

I remember the last time The Other Me appeared, or at least the part of me that isn't bogged down by the aftermath remembers.

A tragic event I will recount another day, but one that left me a broken shell of a person desperate to release myself from the world I was doomed to wander in. I recall getting into my car, shirt and jeans still soaked with blood and driving down the motorway on autopilot, my sole thought droning in my skull like an incantation: "How can I crash this car without hurting anyone else?" It was almost normal in that moment of psychosis to see The Other Me staring in the rear-view mirror, perched on my backseat, and punching itself in the face. Nothing about it resembled me anymore. Not in skin tone, eyes, smile, or even form. It was a jumbled mess, like someone pushed *Random* in an RPG character creation and stretched the proportions until they went beyond comical and became downright uncomfortable to look at.

I barely recognised it for a moment, confused at its appearance until it leaned forward and whispered in my ear, a distorted voice with barely any familiarity to it slithering into my ear:

"Where are you going?" I kept my hands gripped onto the steering wheel as my heart beat faster, short glances in the mirror while the night road unfurled in front of me.

"I don't know." I replied, voice barely above a whisper. I'd spent the last 6 hours sobbing and screaming. There simply wasn't much left. "Did you ever know? I did." It clutched at something in its free arm, out of sight. "Look at the cars passing by. Every one of them knows where they are going. But not you, not anymore." I don't know if it was the psychosis, the lack of self-preservation or the desire to have something bad happen to me, but my fear gave way just enough to face this monstrosity head on. "What are you?

All my life you've showed up at the worst moments. I'm no closer to understanding you now than I was 20 years ago. So, tell me… You owe me that much." It laughed. A coarse, dry wheeze that felt like it was splitting my skin.

"Would giving you one of the many names affixed to me help in any way? Would naming me bring you some comfort? No, there is no point in that. So instead, I will show you." It raised up its free hand, something swaddled in its arm from head to toe. I knew immediately what it was and had to do everything in my power not to slam on the brakes.

I watched as the lifeless shape dwindled in its palm until nothing but soil, insects, and flowers remained. For a brief moment, someone's face flashed upon The Other's, and I recognised it. In that instant, it melted away and was replaced with the unfamiliar once more.

"Do you hear something burning?" It asked, a mixture of mockery and bitterness in its voice. "I am not one thing, but two."

The light of a door opening behind it blinded me as my car swerved. I slammed on the breaks to counter, hearing the screaming blare of a horn as something smashed into my vehicle and sent me into darkness.

## IX

I kept the light close to me as we walked through the cavern. I expected the natural sounds of dripping moisture, rocks moving under my feet, and maybe even a bat or two skittering around. Instead, I felt as if I were walking down a sterile hallway made of obsidian, no discernible life sentient or otherwise beyond me and Bastion, who refused to walk further ahead than myself.

I thought about everything that led to this moment, to the magnitude of this discovery. The more I ruminated on it, the harder it was to believe I'd gotten here so quickly and with such little issue… had it really been 10 years? It almost felt like…

Bastion barked and licked my hand for comfort as he sensed something up ahead. I stopped and unfurled the book for the next instruction: "Your mettle shall be tested now that you have appeased the lord's beast and stepped into the tunnel between your home and his. Once you reach the sea of doors, trust your memento to pick the right one. Do not be swayed by other doors of alluring light and familiarity. They harbour nothing of worth or joy behind them." Another inscription beneath it: The roots are black, and they blot out the sun. The days blur together. Why? The burning grows every day.

I continued on, roughly 10 more minutes of walking in this tunnel that often felt as if I were walking on air. Eventually, the light shone on a small archway that looked eerily similar to the same one I'd seen in my mirror constantly throughout my life, albeit absent of any spectre of doorway lord.

Stepping through it, I realised how vast this cavern was. With my flashlight above me, I could see tens of thousands of archways, just like the one I stood on, littered across the walls of this endless cave. Floating around them like fireflies were an equally innumerable number of doors, seemingly drawn to the archways like moths to a flame before swiftly moving onto the next.

As I stood there with Bastion loyally sat by my side, multiple doors flew down to get my attention, A bright red mahogany door that looked eerily similar to that of my first loves home, my university dorm room where some of my best times were spent, a hospital room I wished to never see again…

On and on they went, many I knew, and some that had long since faded from memory. Eventually, the door I was inexorably drawn to was the one I knew I'd been seeking all along.

A black and white oaken wood door, a small vertical windowpane in the centre and a thick black knocker on the front with the number "47" across the front.

This was it, my childhood home.

It stopped in front of me and hummed softly as I grabbed the handle and pulled it back with me until it fit into the archway, a soft piano tune emanating from the other side. Lilting and familiar, but not quite able to place.

I checked the book again: "Your door has been chosen, now it is up to you to take the final steps forward. This is uncharted territory for each pilgrim, but we must caution you about overstaying your welcome. Do not linger and do not interact. You will awaken something that seeks to keep you here." And another inscription beneath it: Anger. Confusion. Fog. Embers.

The sound of something burning rippled through the cavern, faint popping and crackling sounds inter-splicing with the gentle hum of the door and the delicate piano keys from behind it.

I gripped the handle tightly and stepped through.

# X

The road to recovery is one rife with pitfalls, difficulties of a physical, mental, and emotional form that can cripple the strongest and most fastidious of rehabilitators.

But what mends the body cannot always mend the mind. Trauma is a wound that doesn't heal correctly. It is a fire burning through kindling at an expedient pace and eventually the holes it leaves behind grow until the burn has spread like a cancer, infecting your everyday life, and turning bright skies black and all forms of enjoyment mute and mundane.

Eventually, when the grief and struggle become too much to bear, all you want to do is see the journey end.

But a journey full of intrigue and mystique is often one we don't ruminate over. We forget that our feet hurt, our eyes sting from tiredness and our stomachs ache from hunger. Instead, we relish in the beauty of our surroundings, the serenity of the quiet moments on our travels, and the sanctity of mindfulness when able to think with clarity.

Alas, once the journey is over, much of that can fall to the wayside as the end comes into view and the melancholy of the aftermath rears its ugly head.

And we are reminded, with the same crushing weight from the first time it was relayed to us, that all things must eventually end. All flames turn to embers, and everything return to the soil.

What is left is nothing short of blissful silence ambling its way to the finish line.

# XI

I knew where I was the moment I stepped through the doorway. The smell of a summer's BBQ wafting in from the garden. I can't explain how, but it felt like the early 2000s, a staple of bygone days when everything made sense.

I was in my childhood home. The doorway had brought me where I wanted to go.

It'd brought me home.

I stepped through the porch as Bastion bounded off ahead of me, excited to explore and seemingly right at home in a place he'd never been to before. Perhaps he sensed my own comfort.

Walking through the living room, I noticed all the curtains were drawn, and no daylight shone through. A nighttime BBQ certainly wasn't out of the question, but it was certainly odd.

I traversed through the home until I came to the conservatory connecting my kitchen to the garden.

I have never seen a spectacle such as what I gazed upon at that moment.

The garden, localised in its own cosmic bio-dome, the sky above littered with fireflies and a gentle breeze. But beneath my feet stood a cosmic dance of unquantifiable proportions, stars dancing with one another, cradled in nebulas that stretched on forever and burst into beautiful colours.

It was creation itself. It was beautiful.

"You like the view? It rarely ever gets dull." I looked up to see my dad, sat in a deck chair with a glass of brandy and a smile on his face. No injuries, no vacant stare, just the man my dad used to be.

"I'm sure you have questions, but it'd be best if you sat down first. It'll make the process easier."

I obliged and caught sight of a shooting star underneath our feet, rushing across the cosmos to get to an unknown destination. On its path to somewhere great, no doubt.

Looking at my dad properly, I couldn't believe my luck, that the book had been right.

"Where… where are we? I mean, I know it's home, but…" I gestured around me, trying, and failing, to find the words.

Dad smiled, no dent in his skull or droop in his lip.

"Well, you might call it a halfway home. I know it's referred to by many things amongst many people. My neighbours call it perdition, for example. But it's just where we all wait." He looked up and marvelled at the fireflies overhead, softly twinkling as unseen crickets clicked away. "It isn't so bad, I suppose. Barney helps pass the time."

I blinked, realising I'd not seen him since I came in. Dad seemed to register my confusion and leaned forward, that knowing look in his eyes.

"Something on my face, Dad?" I joked, but he didn't laugh.

"Where did you get Bastion, T.J.?"

I thought for a moment, trying to make sense of the rush of emotions.

"Oh, some rescue shelter, it was… man, I can't remember anymore, but they were nice. Why?"

Dad stared ahead, eyes glistening. "How old is he?"

"I…"

My mind went blank. Why couldn't I remember?

I heard the pitter patter of his footsteps and turned as if to confirm I wasn't going mad, that by somehow looking at him I'd activate that part of my brain and confirm his age.

Instead, I was looking at my childhood dog, Barney. No mistaking it, his goofy smile, slightly overweight build, constantly messy mane from nervously chewing on it whenever he got scared…

"Where are you living now, son?" Dad pressed, turning my attention back to him as the sky overhead grew red, a feeling of foreboding growing within me.

"A little cabin somewhere… I think… I don't understand why you're asking…" I felt uneasy, as if something was pushing its way to the surface of my mind. An image rippled into my head of a slew of pills on my nightstand, soft lilting music and the feeling of floating…

"Son, you are not supposed to be here. This is not a place for someone like you. If The Other catches you…" His lip quivered and my eyes widened in shock. "They are always looking for more prisoners, more bodies to snatch. They want your life, and they'll do ANYTHING to have it. But worst still, If IT finds out you're here…"

"What finds me? What are you talking about? Is there no treasure beyond this?" I stood up, heart pounding in my chest as the last 10 years of searching for the book, time with bastion, living in the log cabin and everything in between began to flash in my mind, burning my skull.

Then he hugged me. The sort that you give after a long-awaited reunion. The sort that softens the unbearable pain of loss.

"I'm giving you the greatest treasure of all, Theo. I'm giving you another chance at life."

I remembered. Like a lightning bolt rushing up my spine, I saw the sky match the crimson red of my blood boiling as images of grief, rage and self-loathing rippled across my mind. The decision to end it all with meds and soft music seeming like a lifetime ago. How long had it been?

I realised I was crying, Barney nuzzling my hand and softly whimpering.

"Wait, but that means… Will I forget? I don't… I don't want to forget." I could barely contain my sobs. "I just got here. I just got to see you as… You. It's the one thing I wanted to see above all else."

He chuckled softly. "Maybe that's why your journey ended here, your treasure."

"Fuck…what happens now?"

"You're going to wake up. It's going to hurt like nothing else. Your body will resent you, give it time to understand and love it like you never have before. I wish I could be there, but this is the best I can do." I felt a crackling noise and a shaking beneath my feet, but in that moment, I didn't care as I hugged him back. "You made your journey here for a reason. It isn't over yet."

"I swear, I will keep your memory alive. I will never let it fade. No matter what happens." I sobbed into his shoulder as something rippled in the room and we broke away.

The book's proclamation rang out in my mind like an alarm bell as something unspeakable tore its way into Dad's personal prison, reaching for me with a hand the size of an oak tree.

"Do not linger and do not interact. You will awaken something that seeks to keep you here."

I had just enough time to kiss Barney on the forehead before bolting for the door. Taking one last glimpse at my dad's face before reality again crushed me with the ugly truth.

He was smiling from ear to ear.

## XII

Vascular Dementia has another name affixed to it and its sibling afflictions: The Cruel Disease.

My Father has bounced back from brain injury after brain injury for 11 years. Every single time the end was in sight, he proved them wrong. He defeated Death itself and came back with a smile on his face.

But death is nothing if not a vengeful beast that dislikes being cheated.

One too many injuries and father time caught up and his diagnosis was finalised not too long ago. His decline went from steady to rapid in the last few months, now reaching a point where he is a shell of his former self, often confused and rarely present.

To say it's heart-breaking to watch and care for is a severe understatement and if there was one thing I desperately wish was relegated to the world of fantasy, it is this.

The more burdens got affixed to my already weary shoulders, the harder it got to even get out of bed with the crushing weight, let alone commit to routine tasks.

Do you understand what I'm saying?

I'll say little of my recovery following the wake-up. For it was as all unsuccessful attempts at ending one's life are painful, embarrassing and with a painful road to recovery and eventual self-love, even if that feels like a mountain to traverse.

Instead, I want to tell you about my dad. About the man affectionately known as "Switch" because of his short stature. I don't get it either, but it's endearing.

My Dad was a voracious reader, and he always loved the hero's journey, the struggle, and the eventual overcoming of obstacles to get the coveted prize.

Perhaps that's why it left such an indelible mark on me and the way my brain worked while I was stuck in that other place.

I visited him recently. He was sitting in his chair and idly watching television, the damage his mind had gone through now visible on his face, his frame shrunk and largely vacant stares.

He is now between Stages 5 and 6.

"Hey Dad, I hope you're doing okay…"

Nothing initially, sometimes his bouts of confusion and non-communication could go on for a while, so while it hurt, it wasn't unexpected.

I sat down and watched him for a while, wondering what was going on in his head. After some time, I broke the silence.

"I wrote about a journey I went on, you know. It was pretty exciting. I'm sure you'd have loved it…"

Something in him lit up, his eyes bright and a childlike glee on his face as he turned to me expectantly.

"Would you mind telling me what happened?"

"Are you sure? It's a little on the long-winded side. I know how you hate things that go on and on…"

"Well, the way I see it, we have all the time in the world. Given the unique place we're in."

"The unique place? Where are you referring to?"

He smiled, almost knowingly. The fog of confusion lifted and the man he once was shining through.

"At the end of our time, we are everywhere."

# ACKNOWLEDGEMENTS

All my love to my parents Julia and Rod. What time we have left is beyond precious to me and the gratitude I have for anything we get beyond that is immeasurable. Thank you for always supporting me.

Jerry, Jai, Ash: My brothers. We are four kings looking to change the landscape of our art form. We'll do it one bit at a time. I wouldn't be the person I am without your guidance. Thank you.

Olie and Tim: For helping me keep my head on straight and a shoulder to cry on. Forever grateful to you both. PTB.

Misty: My sister from another mister. Has it really been 25 years of friendship? You, like a handful of others, helped inspire the skeleton of this novella and I will always be grateful for the day you stepped into my life in kindergarten. Thank you for never leaving.

Bonnie: I couldn't ask for a better writing collaborator and friend. You have never stopped believing in me, championing my work, and we got to watch our universes take off together. I am so proud of everything the campgrounds has and will achieve. Thank you for being a part of Sturgeon.

Sam, Mark, Kay, Des, Hanmer, Jordy, Nat, Kieran: For all the laughs, long gaming sessions and longer chats. Thank you.

To everyone we lost, those we couldn't save, and those who are at peace after a lifelong war with their demons: You will always be loved, and you will always be honoured.

To all of you who pre-ordered: Be it in Kindle format, physical copy, or signed... Thank you for believing in me.

To my readers: Whether you were on the train with *The Bar Series* 2 years ago, *The Last Sin Eater* 1 year ago or you found me last week. I appreciate you. Nearly 4,000 of you showing your appreciation in so many wonderful ways. I do not deserve such a beautiful, kind and diverse fanbase. I will continue to do right by you to the best of my ability.

And for Clara, my little light who will live forever. This is for you. I will always love you.

9 781963 107074